FINDING HERSELF

Sandhya Rajasekhar

Contents

Acknowledgement   v

Chapter One: Mother   1

Chapter Two: Growing Up   17

Chapter Three: The Marriage   26

Chapter Four: College   38

Chapter Five: The Village   47

Chapter Six: The New Arrival   56

Chapter Seven: The Decision   70

Chapter Eight: The Project   83

Chapter Nine: Anupama   95

Chapter Ten: A New Beginning   108

Epilogue   117

Acknowledgement

S ome words of gratitude are in order: thanks to V. M. Rajasekhar and Deepa Makesh for their initial editing; Sathyabama Oppili for being the first one to read a partially complete manuscript and giving me the thumbs up, and all the others who read the story and gave a positive response. Thanks and love to Parinita for her encouragement, and Harini for giving me the final impetus to publish the story. All thanks to Harini for the cover ideation and illustration. My thanks to the creative team that refined the cover and the editorial team at Notion Press. Many thanks to Duraiya Fakhruddin at Notion Press for her patience.

CHAPTER ONE

Mother

S he wished she could tear that day into pieces. "And throw it in the waste basket," she muttered to herself. Just the way her brother tore up sheets of paper when angry. "And got spankings from *amma*!" Anupama could not help giggling at the memory.

***

Her English class was on when it happened. She saw Sarala at the door and knew the time had come. She had expected it, of course, but could not help wishing she could die, too, and join her mother. Sarala squeezed her hand gently, and tears rushed to her eyes. Her mother had been seriously injured when a lorry rammed into their car. *Appa* recovered soon, but *amma* never did. The house was silent when she entered it. She held Sarala's hand tightly for support. She could not bear to look at her father, Raghunath, or her brother, Venkat, who sat by her mother's side. There was no way she could look at her mother, freshly bathed and covered in a clean white sheet.

"Saralakka," she gasped almost inaudibly, "May I go to my room?"

She put her head on the table and sobbed in the privacy of her room. Why did *amma* have to go? "Where are you,

Amma?" she cried out loud. She sobbed until she was too tired to even cry. Sarala came into her room. "Do I have to?" asked Anupama without waiting for her to speak.

"Come, *Putti.*" Anupama clasped Sarala's hand tightly as she walked into the hall to pay her last respects to her mother. Her heart beat so loud, she thought it would explode. She did not look up at anyone; she was oblivious to her father, her brother, her mother's parents, friends, and relatives who had gathered around. She clasped her mother's feet and bowed, her head touching them, her heart filled with love and sadness. "Goodbye, *Amma,*" she whispered.

Sarala walked her back to the privacy of her room. "I don't want to come out again, Saralakka," she requested. She did not know it when they took away her mother.

It was evening when she felt a gentle shake on her shoulder. "Have something to eat, *Putti.*" Anupama looked up anxiously at Sarala. "Have they all gone, Saralakka? What about *amma?*" "They have taken Lathakka to her final resting place. Now drink this, Anno," Sarala held a glass of milk to her mouth.

"*Amma* has gone? Where? To God?"

Sarala ran her fingers through her hair. "Yes, *Putti.*"

To God. So that was it. When her grandfather died, her mother had told her the same thing. "That means she will never come back again," her brain screamed.

Fresh tears streamed down her cheeks. "But why? Doesn't she love me and Venki and *appa?* She told me she would never leave us!"

Amma: Mother, *Putti:* Little one, *Akka:* Older sister

Sarala did her best to console the eight-year-old child. She gently persuaded her to have a glass of milk and helped her into bed. Only after Anupama fell asleep did she leave the room.

Anupama did not dare go to school the next day. She stayed in her room, refusing to meet anybody. She could hear her brother accusing their father in the next room, and the soft comforting voices of her grandparents, who had lost their only daughter.

It was afternoon. Sarala had forced her to eat. She was sitting up in bed thinking of her mother, school, and homework when her brother came in. She looked up at him and said quietly, "It was not *appa*'s fault, and you know it, Venki."

Venkat sat down by her side. She continued, "Why do you want to hurt *appa* like that? He is already so sad."

"So am I!" Venkat blurted angrily.

That evening, her best friend, Soumya, dropped in. Soumya was her neighbour and classmate. Both girls hit it off at the very first meeting as toddlers and were now quite inseparable.

"Hi, Anno, why didn't you come to school today?"

When Soumya's family moved to Mysore, Latha met them as neighbours, and a two-year-old Anupama had introduced herself by stretching out her name in a sing-song voice, "Annopamaa." And since then, she was Anno to everyone close to her.

Anupama looked up anxiously at Sarala who had let Soumya in. "Saralakka, didn't you send a leave letter with Soumya?"

Appa: Father, *Anna*: Brother.

"Yes, and it was for one day's leave only," Sarala said firmly. "Venkat *anna* is also going tomorrow," she added, and that settled the issue.

Soumya took Anupama by the hand and pulled her out into the garden. Both girls disappeared into Soumya's house. Anupama returned with her friend's class notebooks and was soon busy copying the day's notes. Being studious and intelligent, she completed her homework in no time. "*Amma* will be happy," she thought, nodding her head with satisfaction.

School was not as bad as she thought it would be. Her friends were very nice to her, and her teachers did not trouble her with questions about her mother. Lunchtime was great, with her friends offering her the best part of their food.

After school, Anupama and Soumya got into the school bus and reached home. The two girls got off the bus at Anupama's house, threw down their bags on the front porch steps, and sat down to do their homework. Meanwhile, Sarala, who had heard the bus, opened the door for them.

Homework over, Anupama said "bye" to her friend and got into the house. It was then that the truth hit her once again. The house was quiet. She hesitated as she entered the cool drawing room. "Saralakka? Where are you? Don't you know I'm home?" she called out, not daring to look at her mother's room.

Her grandmother called out to her from her mother's room, and Anupama walked towards it hesitantly. Of course, she did not expect to see her mother there, but it all felt so strange. She walked in and sat by her father's side. Her grandmother was holding her mother's jewels. "These are my mother's," she was saying, "And I gave them to Latha at her wedding." She turned to Anupama. "Now they are yours," she said. Her mother's chains and earrings and bangles! How often had she tried them on and preened in front of the mirror, much to her mother's amusement! Each piece brought to mind a special memory of her mother.

She hugged the box to herself. "Can I keep this in my almirah? Please? And *amma's* sarees, too. I don't want anyone to touch them." Her father only smiled and ran his fingers through her hair. Finally, her mother's almirah was shifted to her bedroom. Anupama was thrilled. She had a part of *amma* to herself! She would not allow it to be taken away from her room, ever.

Anupama's grandparents left two weeks later, back to their lives in Bangalore. Life slowly limped back to its old ways. Sarala and Soumya saw to it that Anupama went to school and did her homework right from day one. Venkat, seven years her senior, was in tenth grade.

"A surprise gift," her father would say about her birth.

"And a most welcome one," her mother never failed to add.

***

Anupama sighed. It was now almost three months. Thank God for Saralakka. Thank God granny sent her when *amma* was ill. She did not know much about Saralakka. Her grandmother's distant relative from the village or someone to that effect. Anyway, all that mattered to her was that she was a nice lady and looked after the house and all of them.

***

Three months after her mother passed away, they went to her father's house in the village, just about an hour and a half away from Mysore, where they lived. His mother had been too old and weak to visit them, and while Raghunath did visit her earlier, the children were here now that their exams were over. Her father's brother Ramnath and his wife, who couldn't come when her mother passed away, had come down from the US.

The sorrow on her grandmother's face was too much for Anupama to bear. She escaped into the shady and quiet garden whenever she could. Lying on the hammock that hung between two mango trees, she could dream of her mother. And her mother always appeared to her, bright and beautiful.

"How come you are so beautiful, *Amma?*" Anupama would sometimes ask her mother. At which her mother would laugh and say, "Because you love me!" Anupama wondered what *amma* meant by that.

A spider had made a large web in the branches of one of the mango trees. Anupama hoped the spider wouldn't crawl down and bite her. It might be poisonous! But then, *amma* had once told her while they were lazing in the same garden that not all spiders were poisonous.

Amma knew everything, thought the little girl. She always had an answer to all her queries.

Why, she even helped Venki with his Science and Maths subjects!

The little girl shed fresh tears of sorrow for her mother. 'God, send my mother back to me, please. I promise to be a good girl and study well,' she cried.

She ran into the house, crawled into her grandmother's bed, and fell asleep next to her grandmother, who was having her afternoon nap.

***

Nobody disturbed Anupama when she lay on the hammock, dreaming of her mother. Sarala wandered around the garden sometimes but left Anupama alone. One afternoon, eyeing another spider's web, Anupama muttered, "Saralakka, grandma's garden is full of spiders."

"But not all of them are poisonous, so don't worry," replied Sarala.

That was just what *amma* had said! She looked at Sarala with more respect than usual. "How do you know? Do you read a lot too, like *amma* used to?"

"I just happen to know, that's all," smiled Sarala.

"Have you gone to college, Saralakka? Like *amma* and Lakshmi auntie from the US?"

"No, *Putti*, but I did finish my schooling, yes."

Anupama wanted to know more. She asked, "But why not? Didn't you like going to college?"

"I wanted to, my dear. But my father got me married."

The little girl's eyes widened with surprise. "Married? Then where is *anna*?" she asked, referring to Sarala's husband.

Sarala sighed. "He died soon after we married, many years ago, *Putti*." Only 25, Sarala was married at 17 and widowed at 18. The shock had made her deliver a stillborn child, two months after her husband's death.

There was silence. After some time, Anupama asked softly, "Do you miss him, Saralakka? Like I miss *amma*?"

"Yes, I do," said Sarala. Nobody had asked her that before. "But time is a great healer."

What does she mean, wondered Anupama. She felt a sort of kinship with Sarala and decided to be nicer to her in the future. From now on, she would eat without fussing too much, she thought.

That night, lying next to her grandmother, Anupama asked, "*Ajji*, where is Saralakka's house?"

"In the next village, her father is coming tomorrow. Did you know?"

Saralakka's father! Anupama was curious, "What does he do? Is he a farmer?"

Her grandmother mumbled a sleepy "yes" and told her to close her eyes and sleep.

***

Chinnappa, a poor farmer, was a distant cousin of Anupama's grandmother. He worked on a small farm and lived in a small thatched house with his widowed daughter, Sarala. Things got better when Sarala went to the city to look after Raghunath's children. Raghunath sent him a good sum of money every month.

***

Anupama was lazing in the garden when she heard her grandmother call out to her. "Ah, Anno, there you are," she said when Anupama came running into the room, "this is Saralakka's father, Chinnappa, my cousin." Anupama looked curiously at Chinnappa, tall, bent, his serious face lightened by warm eyes.

Sarala was happy, too.

Ajji: Grandmother

"So, you are Anupama," he said with a friendly smile, "Sarala has told me a lot about you." Sarala came in with her bag, "Bye, *Putti*, I will see you soon." Seeing the quizzical look on Anupama's face, she smiled and added, "And yes, I will come back with you to the city." She bid an affectionate goodbye and left with her father.

The next few days were quite boring for Anupama. A visit to her grandmother's house was something all of them looked forward to every year. Her mother loved the serenity and greenery. Grandma's house would be full of light and laughter and good food. They went on picnics to nearby places or just walked down to the river. Venki and she used to try catching fish or just play around in the water. Her mother always joined them at such times, much to Anupama's joy.

She suddenly realised that nobody laughed or spoke much since *amma* went. Venki, who loved meeting childhood friends in the village, kept to himself. He was always reading. Sometimes, he walked down to the river alone. *Appa* had already gone back home, which now seemed dark and dreary to her.

Anupama sat next to her grandmother in the evenings on the verandah. A soft-natured and affectionate woman, the old lady told Anupama about her mother's first visit to the village house and how beautiful she looked as a bride. She realised how lost the little girl felt without her mother and grieved more for the child than for anyone else. Anupama also learned to confide in her grandmother and asked her endless questions about her mother.

***

Raghunath and Latha studied together in college and went on to do their postgraduation in Business Administration together as well. They were placed in the same company after their Masters and decided that the best way to continue to be together was to get married.

Raghunath and she were both 24 when they married. Venkat was born a year after the wedding. They were thrilled and excited to welcome Anupama to their world seven years later.

***

Anupama did not then realise how much her conversations with her grandmother helped her. But by the time she left for home, there was some peace within her and a quiet confidence to face life without the person she loved the most in the world. She felt the presence of her mother everywhere; her mother was in her heart and in her mind. As time passed by, that presence was to be more comforting than painful, though the void left by her mother's death did not get filled.

***

She and her father were caring towards each other. Anupama was always gentle and affectionate with her father, but now the carefree laughter between them had disappeared. Venki was extremely protective towards his kid sister, but a wall seemed to have appeared between him and his father. And that was something the little girl could do nothing about.

Saralakka's presence was a big relief to Anupama. The two of them soon developed a great friendship, and it was only her company that helped Anupama get back to her old cheerful self.

Going to school was something she looked forward to every morning. She would lose herself in her lessons and games. Soumya and she stuck together. She was more welcome than ever in Soumya's house and was glad of the attention she got there, especially from Soumya's mother, Kamala auntie.

Anupama and Venki were soon in the thick of school, tests, and exams.

***

Her father returned home early these days. He looked forward to teaching his daughter and spending time with her. It was a whole new experience for both of them.

Sarala became more and more a part of the family. Anupama could not dream of life without her.

Sarala was a great storyteller, and Anupama loved to listen to her as she told a tale. "You seem to read a great deal, Saralakka," she remarked one day, "but you don't read English, do you?"

"There is so much to read in one's own language. I don't think I am missing much."

"But Saralakka! Tintin? Asterix? Nancy Drew?"

Sarala laughed. She knew Anupama was referring to the books she was glued to after her homework and studies for the day were over.

"From tomorrow on, we are going to have English classes here in my room," said Anupama firmly.

And she kept her word.

***

It was Sunday. Venkat, who was now doing his plus two, had gone for his Mathematics tuition.

Anupama was bored. Sarala, who was having her afternoon nap, suggested sleepily, "Why don't you and *anna* go for a movie?"

"Go for a movie with *appa*?" Anupama was shocked. There had been no music, no movies, and no outings ever since her mother died. The car, after coming from the garage, stood in the portico, gathering dust. Her father had not driven it since the accident.

"Why not?" asked Sarala quietly, "Lathakka wouldn't mind at all. I am sure she'll be very happy for your sake."

Anupama slowly walked back to her room.

What fun they used to have, going for movies! Movie and dinner. *Amma* enjoyed comedies. Shah Rukh Khan was her favourite. "Yes, going for a movie is a good idea," thought Anupama. "What will *appa* say? And Venki?" But the more she thought about it, the more it seemed like a good idea. After all, even *appa* needed a break.

She woke her father up and told him she wanted to see the latest Hindi movie in town. Her father was relieved. He had been worrying about her. She had become too quiet and withdrawn.

After tea, the two of them got dressed and stepped out. Anupama ran to the gates and opened them.

"Why don't we take a bus, Anno," suggested her father.

"But why? I want to go by car," Anupama said.

"Ok, so be it," said her father and went into the house to get the keys.

✳✳✳

It was past nine when they got back home. Venkat was waiting anxiously at the gate.

He quickly opened the gates to let the car in.

Once inside the house, he shouted at his father. "Whose idea was it? How could you go for a movie? And that too by car! You are not taking Anupama in the car again!"

Anupama's heart beat so fast, she thought it would burst. "But Venki, I wanted to go by car."

"You? Have you forgotten how *amma* died? And what made you go for a movie? Have you already stopped missing *amma*?"

Pale and trembling, Anupama stammered, "But Saralakka said…"

Venki shook her by the shoulders. "Saralakka? Who is she to tell us anything…"

Their father interrupted. "That's enough, Venki. I took Anno to a movie because she wanted to. And she has every right to lead a normal life."

"Normal life? You took that all away from us, didn't you?" Venkat ran into his room and banged the door shut.

Anupama felt wretched. Her heart went out to her father who had walked into his room. She followed him inside and hugged him, saying "It is okay, *Appa*, don't feel so bad." She looked up at him with eyes full of sympathy. "From now on, you are taking me out in the car, okay? I was not at all afraid," she declared, as her father gently ran his fingers through her hair.

They had a quiet dinner. Venki did not turn up at the table. Nobody dared call him, either.

Later, when Sarala came to her room, Anupama apologised. "Saralakka," she said timidly. "I am sorry about what Venki said."

Sarala smiled. "Forget it, *Putti*. What matters is that you enjoyed the evening and got your father to drive that car again."

Anupama felt relieved and chatted excitedly. "You know, the movie was great fun. I really enjoyed it. *Amma* would have liked it too."

That night, for the first time since her mother's death, Anupama went to sleep with a smile on her lips. "Good night, *Amma*," she said in her mind, "I love you."

***

From then on, Raghunath took his daughter out for drives whenever possible. It was wonderful to have his little daughter trust his capabilities, despite the tragedy in their lives. He spent time with her every evening and involved himself completely in her studies, something he had taken for granted when Latha was there. Anupama responded eagerly to her father's attempts at trying to fill the void created by her mother's absence.

"No studies for me today, *Appa*," she announced one day.

Sarala came into the room with tea for them. "I am taking a test today," she smiled.

"Test?" What test?"

"English! I am giving Saralakka a test in spoken and written English," declared Anupama. "You see, I am her English teacher."

Her father laughed. She was so much like her mother. "Great. Finish your homework first."

But Venki became more and more withdrawn. Raghunath respected his son's feelings, though it upset him. Venki spent all his time at home with his books, which was a relief. He was studious and intelligent and wanted to become an engineer. He had important exams ahead of him, and Raghunath realised that the best thing to do at this time was to leave him alone.

Coming home from school one day, Anupama was surprised to hear music coming from her brother's room.

Venkat gave her a small smile when she ran into his room. "*Amma's* favourite cassette."

That night, as she got ready to go to bed, Sarala asked Anupama, "Didn't Lathakka listen to our songs at all?"

"Of course, Saralakka. But you see, the Beatles were her favourite."

"Beatles? You mean those insects?" Sarala, who was learning English with great interest, asked with a mischievous smile.

Anupama enjoyed the joke and laughed, "You know, Saralakka, even dad used to call them that, just to tease *amma*! But seriously. Haven't you seen *amma's veena*? She used to enjoy playing that. She even taught me how to play *Sa Re Ga Ma.*"

"Then how come I have not seen you play it?" asked Sarala.

Anupama did not reply. The next evening, when her father returned from work, she asked him if she could play the *veena* because Saralakka wanted to hear her play *Sa Re Ga Ma* the way *amma* had taught her.

"Of course, sweetheart," her father replied, thanking Sarala in his mind. The credit for keeping his daughter cheerful and bright, he knew, went to Sarala. Thank God Chinnappa agreed to send his daughter here, he thought,

A week later, Sarala told Raghunath that Soumya's mother knew of a music school where they taught the *veena*. "She says she will send Soumya, too, if Anno goes."

"Why not? But you will have to accompany them."

Anupama and Soumya were most excited. Sarala took them to the *veena* class three times every week from then on.

Veena: Indian stringed musical instrument.

Sa Re Ga Ma: The first notes in Indian classical music.

CHAPTER TWO

Growing Up

Once school closed for yet another summer, Sarala went to her house in the village for a few days. Raghunath took his daughter to the home of her maternal grandparents, where she would spend the first part of her holidays. She was to spend the rest of the holidays in her father's ancestral house in the village, and then get back home. Venkat's results were out, and he passed with distinction. He was too busy to accompany her to the village. There were more exams to follow. "Entrance exams," he told his sister, who shook her head in wonderment. He wanted to be an engineer and go to the US like Ram uncle.

Anupama was extremely fond of her grandparents, and she had become dearer to them after their daughter's death. Anupama wanted to use the room that her mother used as a girl, all by herself this time.

"This is going to be my room from now on," she declared.

Her grandfather left for work in the mornings, and throughout the day, she had only her grandmother for company. They spent most of their free time going through old albums.

Her mother had collected so many books and magazines! Even the ones she read as a little girl were there, all neatly arranged in a row, old and worn out, but still readable. And her collection of Amar Chitra Kathas, all nicely bound, was just out of this world! Anupama was soon lost in the world of books.

Living in her grandparents' house, having her mother's room all to herself, was a new adventure for her. She opened every little cupboard, every little book and envelope in the room, hoping to find more and more of her mother. She felt her mother's warm loving presence everywhere, and many times wished that her holidays would never end, even though she missed her *appa*, Venki, and Saralakka. Her mother's room became her refuge from the outside world from then on.

At last, it was time to go. Anupama's grandparents took her to her father's house in the village, where her lonely grandmother waited for her. Her grandparents left two days later.

***

Her hammock was back in its old place. Anupama spent most of her time there, lazing, thinking, reading, and dreaming in the shade.

She wondered if Saralakka would come visiting. How good that would be! She realised that she missed her a lot. She jumped out of the hammock and ran to her grandmother to find out. Chinnappa was there, talking to her grandmother, but Saralakka was not there.

"How are you, Anupama?" Chinnappa asked when he saw her. "Sarala will be here in two days."

Seeing the disappointed look on her face, he said, "Would you like to come home with me? Sarala will be thrilled."

Saralakka's house! Anupama was agog with excitement. Jumping with joy, she begged her grandmother to let her go.

Soon after lunch, Anupama, all packed for a two-day stay, was ready to leave. Her grandmother insisted that Chinnappa leave in the family car. Sarala's house was about an hour and a half's drive from her grandmother's house. As she neared the house, she saw with delight that the river flowed there, too. What fun!

Anupama did not know that life was also lived like this. There were no taps in the bathroom or toilet! How was she to spend two days there? She forgot all about it when Sarala took her to the river that evening. They played and bathed in the river and returned home, happy and exhausted.

Sarala woke her up early the next morning. "Come on, I will take you to the river."

She had had her breakfast and was ready to go.

They had a good wash in the river. She played about in the water trying to catch the colourful tiny fishes darting around her, while Sarala washed their clothes.

Lunch was a simple meal of rice and fish curry. The fish was caught by Chinnappa in the river, as a treat for his little guest from the city.

***

Chinnappa's cow had just given birth to a calf. After a few tentative trials, Anupama made friends with the little one. She fed it, and sat and talked to it as Sarala milked the cow. Initially worried that the calf may not have enough milk after the milking, she relaxed when she realised that the calf drank to his heart's content every day.

"Would you like to try some milk?" asked Sarala.

"What! Without boiling?" *Amma* would never have allowed that.

"Why not? Taste some fresh milk."

Indeed, it was refreshing! But she decided she preferred boiled milk, any day.

Anupama followed Sarala around the small house. She watched with interest while Sarala worked in the front of the hut, spreading some cow dung and cleaning the area. She then drew a *rangoli*, giving the place a fresh look.

***

Sarala offered to take Anupama to watch a movie at the local theatre. Excited, Anupama got dressed, and they walked down to the theatre.

"But Saralakka! This is not a theatre!"

And indeed, it was not. The last of the village tents stood in front of her, small, quaint, and otherworldly. There were no lines of people waiting to purchase tickets. Sarala bought two tickets at the counter. Anupama looked around in awe. The door was a short rickety one, which led them into the hall with the screen. It was a large empty space with a mud floor and a few chairs at the back. People squatted in the front rows. The hall was warm, filled with noise and chatter. The movie began, and the screen sprang to life. There was a hush as the audience lapped up the magic in silence, broken now and then by applause and cheering.

Anupama chatted excitedly all the way back home. "So, has *amma* been to this tent to watch movies too?" she wanted to know and was elated when Sarala told her that her mother had been there too! "With whom? When? Which movie?" she threw a barrage of questions at Sarala.

They walked in the twilight among mango groves with monkeys here and there. Initially afraid when she saw the monkeys, Anupama relaxed when she saw that Sarala was not perturbed. "Ignore them and do not change your pace," she told Anupama.

Anupama wished Venkat were with her, too. Two days flew by, and it was time to go back to grandma's house. A week later, they were on their way home to Mysore.

***

Soon, Anupama's school reopened, and it was back to school and studies. Venkat passed the entrance exams and was called for admission at IIT Madras. Anupama did not like it at all! She cajoled her brother not to opt for the college in Madras and go for the one in Mysore where he was invited to join.

Venkat comforted his sister, "I will take you around the city whenever you and *appa* visit me." He promised to come as often as possible, too.

Life went on. School went on as usual. Venkat left for his studies at IIT Madras.

Once on an extended weekend holiday, Raghunath suggested they visit Venkat in Madras. He had even booked the tickets without telling Anupama. She was thrilled.

Rangoli: Traditional Indian designs made by connecting dots, using white flour/powdered chalk, that adorn the front of homes.

They left on a night train on Thursday and reached Madras early in the morning. Raghunath had booked a hotel room for them, with an extra bed for Venkat.

Anupama was excited at the thought of going to the beach.

"I can't wait to see the sea!" she squealed, delighted at the alliteration. "See the sea? Did you get that, *Appa*?"

That evening, when Venkat joined them after his classes, they went to the beach. She could hear the waves and smell the water in the air even before they got off the taxi. There were no words to describe her joy! Anupama cupped her face in her hands and looked at the sea with awe. Her brother walked with her to the waters, and they played in the waves until they were tired. They walked back, dragging their feet in the sand, wet and happy. Her father bought her corn on the cob, nicely roasted in the fire, and then they tried shooting balloons.

The beach was dark with firelights here and there, horses trotting up and down, people gathered around the fried fish, *bajji* and corn stalls, hawkers walking around selling boiled groundnuts and chickpeas, balloons, and kites. The waters grew dark till they could no longer see the sea, but only heard its tireless waves. To Anupama, everything was magical; the sea, the beach, and their first real fun outing together after her mother's death.

***

Time flew. Venkat visited them during the holidays, and Anupama eagerly waited for him. Her studies were going well, and soon she was in high school.

Bajji: Savoury fritters

High school was fun; she was part of the school cultural programme. Soumya and she entered their names for as many events as they were allowed to. Evenings were spent practising the dance or song that they were going to perform. Her friends loved practising in her house — Sarala made them delicious snacks to eat! In fact, she kept plates of goodies to eat while the girls practised.

After the eighth-grade exams, Anupama was again dropped off at her mother's place. After that, it was back to her dad's village. Sarala was already there at the village, as usual. She came to stay at Anupama's grandmother's house to help with the guests. This summer was special. Venkat's course was almost getting over, and he decided to spend the summer with his paternal grandmother and Anupama.

Sarala had made a great lunch for Anupama and her grandfather who accompanied her as always. He was staying back for only a day to meet Venkat, who was arriving that night.

'Saralakka, lunch was yummy!' exclaimed Anupama. After lunch, she sat with her grandmother till the old lady fell asleep.

Then off she ran to the garden where Sarala was busy cleaning and clearing. She lay in the hammock and snoozed, waking up now and then when a bird chirped close by. Sarala worked quietly in the garden.

***

During the last week of her stay, her father came so they could all leave together. Anupama noticed that this time her father and grandmother spent a lot of time having serious conversations with each other.

"This is not what I want," she heard her father say once, and always, he shook his head in denial.

Her grandmother was persistent. Anupama saw her wipe her tears once or twice and Raghunath's exasperated look.

Sarala and the children kept away from these conversations. Sarala's father was also part of these discussions once in a while. Sarala left with her father, promising Anupama that she would meet them at the bus stand.

A day before they were to leave for home, Anupama's grandmother called the children to her. "I need to tell you both something. I don't know how much longer I have to live. I cannot leave you both like this. I have convinced your father to marry Sarala. This is in the best interests of everybody," she announced.

It took a while for it to sink in—Anupama was bewildered; she did not know such things could happen, too. Her brother shouted angrily, "No way! You should have asked us before you took such a decision!" He darted an angry look at his father, "Why did you agree without asking us? Weren't we doing fine this way?"

Her grandmother said, "Yes, Venkat. That is why I decided that the arrangement be made permanent. Sarala cannot continue to stay with you all like this forever. It is better for all concerned if they marry. I had to really work hard to convince your father."

Her brother stormed out of the room.

Anupama asked softly, almost to herself, "What about Saralakka?"

"I gave her no choice! And her father is very grateful."

Anupama nodded and followed her brother out of the room.

***

The next few days were nothing short of volatile. Venkat had huge fights with his father. Venkat did not dislike Sarala. As time passed, in fact, his gratitude towards her, especially for the kind caring she showed towards Anupama, turned into respect. He had always been reserved with her; his mother's death hit him hard, and he had no one to share his emotions with. Luckily, he was preoccupied with his studies, and that had helped.

But to accept anyone else in his mother's place! He could not even think of it, let alone accept it. Things were falling into place, and he could not understand why this happened.

"How could you do this, *Ajji*? Please call it off. I will never be part of this."

No amount of tears and cajoling from the old lady could change his mind.

He booked his ticket back to his hostel and left. Anupama was a silent witness to the tension and emotional outbursts between Venkat and her grandmother.

Raghunath cancelled the return tickets. The next few days were a blur of activity. Anupama took no part in it and stayed in her room. Sarala was quiet, too. She remained in the kitchen, cooking for the family. Chinnappa was in a daze, busy getting things ready for the wedding. Anupama's grandmother called for the priest of the village temple and finalised a date – the wedding was to happen in two days! She gave Sarala a few of her silk sarees and her own wedding saree to wear on the occasion. She made phone calls to a few close relatives, inviting them for the wedding.

***

CHAPTER THREE

The Marriage

She was 14 when her father and Saralakka were married.

Raghunath and Sarala were wedded in a simple ceremony at the village temple. His mother was relieved; now she did not have to worry about her son and grandchildren. Raghunath's brother and sister-in-law could not make it from the US for the wedding at such short notice. Chinnappa was flushed with emotion and gratitude. Sarala hardly spoke.

Anupama did not go to the temple.

"No *Ajji*, please leave me alone. I wish I was not in the village at all. How could you do this?" She tearfully accused her grandmother, who tried to cajole her into joining them as they left for the wedding.

Raghunath comforted his old mother. "Leave her alone, let us not force her," he said. He was torn between the logic of his old mother and the distress of his children. He knew Latha would be okay, that his wife would have wanted him to marry again. Latha's parents were relieved when they got the news and gave their consent for the wedding. And now it was too late to back out. He had agreed finally, only because his children were fond of Sarala, who had become a part of the family.

Venkat refused to even consider the marriage.

"I am never coming home," he said with finality as he bid goodbye to Anupama, and she realised he meant it. "I will call you whenever I can. Write to me."

***

Things could never be the same again. Venkat did not come home like he used to whenever he had a long weekend. He preferred to go to his mother's house and spend time with his grandparents during short breaks and holidays.

The warm, trusting friendship and camaraderie between Anupama and Sarala were gone. She was no longer her Saralakka; she had taken the place of her mother. There was more silence and less communication between them now. Anupama grew quiet, withdrawn, and thoughtful.

Her love for her father remained the same, and her regard for Sarala did not diminish. Never did she show in her behaviour or mannerisms the loss she felt; of losing Saralakka as a friend and confidant. She treated her with respect and reserve.

***

Ninth standard had just begun. She was not taking part in this year's sports day drill. It was always Sarala who got her ready with the required drill costume and took her to the stadium an hour earlier, stayed back to watch the drill and other programmes, and got back home with Anupama.

"I will go with my friends to the stadium and get back with them, Saralakka," Anupama said.

Sarala nodded and quietly packed for Anupama something to munch on and a bottle of water.

The stadium was full of chatting students and teachers, as usual. Anupama had a good time with her friends, screaming herself hoarse and cheering with her friends every time her classmates won an event. She came back home, tired and feeling lightheaded. By nighttime, she had a mild fever.

"I don't feel well, *Appa*," she told her father.

"I will make you a soup," said Sarala. She made her some soup, gave her an early dinner and a paracetamol, and made sure she went to bed.

Anupama slept fitfully. She dreamt of her mother and her brother. She was delirious and unaware that Sarala sat in her room tending to her fever with a cold compress.

She felt no better in the morning; she was, in fact, worse. She was nauseous and refused to eat. She puked all over the floor.

"I am sorry," she apologised helplessly as she watched Sarala clean up the mess. It distressed her that Sarala did so much for her.

"It is okay, *Putti*," said Sarala gently.

A worried Raghunath took her to the doctor. The day wore on, and Anupama spent the day in fitful and restless sleep. By the next morning, she seemed better. Sarala was by her bedside whenever possible. One more day's rest and Anupama was good to go to school.

That evening, she came back from school, looking and feeling strange. Sarala was at the door. When Anupama opened the gate and walked in with Soumya, she looked up and caught Soumya's eye. Suddenly, Sarala understood. Yes, of course, that was it.

Anupama was emotional and teary-eyed. She had matured. She knew about it since most of the girls in her group had already attained puberty, and she was privy to all that they went through. It was awkward to have Saralakka around. She missed her mother.

"Can I go to Soumya's house?" she asked, fresh and dressed after a hot bath, preferring the company of her friend and her mother.

Sensing her discomfort, once she left for school the next day, Sarala requested Soumya's mother, Kamala, to take her shopping for new clothes and innerwear.

"I have requested auntie to take you shopping," she informed Anupama once she came from school.

"Thank you, Saralakka. I will be back soon." A greatly relieved Anupama left with Soumya and her mother.

***

Sarala, with her usual quiet industriousness, had learned to read English under Anupama's tutelage. Life was rather lonely after marriage. Raghunath was kind and affectionate, but there was not much talk. Anupama had withdrawn into a shell; she dearly missed her confidential chatter, her warm, trusting friendship. Knowing Anupama, she did not give up hope, though. It was Venkat's disowning of his father that really hurt, and she had to be worth that loss, which she prayed was temporary.

Most of her free time was spent reading, and it soon became her source of relief. Anupama noticed this and borrowed books for her from her school library. Sarala continued to borrow magazines from the small lending library of which Anupama was a member.

***

As a girl, Sarala was a constant visitor at Anupama's grandmother's house. *Chikkamma* always welcomed her warmly and treated her well. Sarala helped in the kitchen and learned many skills and family recipes from her. She helped comb *Chikkamma's* hair, took care of her sarees and clothes, and was the old lady's favourite errand girl.

When Raghunath got married, she was there at the house to welcome the new bride. How beautiful Lathakka looked! Sarala still remembered the first time she saw her. She was soon running errands for her as well and accompanied her whenever she went out in the village. She was there when Venkat and Anupama came there as newborns. The visits became infrequent after her marriage to a farmer from a nearby village. She came back to her father's house and stayed with him after the sudden death of her husband.

Chikkamma called for her and asked her to stay with her. Sarala was unwilling; she wanted to be with her father. She visited the big house every day and took care of the personal needs of the old lady. She took the four o'clock bus back home every evening.

The news of the accident came as a big shock to everyone in the village. The old lady wept many tears. Latha's parents rushed to take care of the children and home.

Chikkamma called for Chinnappa one day and, drying her tears, told him,

"Chinnappa, Latha's condition is bad. The children are struggling. Why don't you send Sarala to stay with them and take care of them? She will be of great help to Raghu."

"So be it, *Akka*. Let her be of some use."

Chikkamma: Younger aunt.

"God bless you, Chinnappa. I shall pay her well."

The old lady called Raghunath over the phone and informed him. Sarala and Chinnappa travelled to the city a week later.

***

Anupama was in her tenth class when her grandmother in the village passed away peacefully in her sleep. They rushed to the village and performed the last rites in their field, with the river flowing nearby. Anupama shed fresh tears, looking into a future that seemed lonelier than ever. Venkat refused to come.

***

Anupama worked hard for her tenth Board exams, and Sarala ensured that she ate well. She served her and Soumya with tea and snacks whenever they did "combined study," as they called it.

Raghunath was grateful, and Anupama never failed to thank Sarala for all her care.

The exams went off well.

Summer came.

"Would you like to come to the village with me?" asked Sarala.

"I would rather go to *ajji's* house in Bangalore. Venki is coming there."

She shrugged and continued, "Also, without *ajji* in the village, it seems weird to go there."

Venkat had finished his degree and had landed a good job in Madras.

Anupama could discern the plea in Sarala's voice. She glanced helplessly at her father.

"I will come too; we will stay for a week. Ask Soumya if she will come with you. She can get back with me," he suggested. "Venky is coming only in a week's time, right? I will put you on the bus from there."

"But of course. That would be great!" Anupama was excited. "I will talk to her now."

She ran out to Soumya's house.

Soumya was thrilled and begged her parents to send her. Her brother Santhosh, four years her senior, agreed to accompany her, at his mother's request.

"Why did we not do this before?!" Anupama and Soumya squealed with excitement as they boarded the bus.

Soumya and she shared her room, and Santhosh was put up in Venkat's. Anupama took them to all the places and houses in the village she frequented. They had a glorious time swimming in the river.

Early in the morning, they walked down to Anupama's grandfather's paddy field, now taken care of by Chinnappa and some cousins of her father's. The two girls dance-walked on the bund, arms held wide out for balance, and laughed uproariously whenever one of them lost balance. The canal bordered their field with that of the next one. There was a small temple there, that of the guardian Goddess. Every day, Chinnappa swept the courtyard and lit the lamp first thing in the morning. The girls sat in the shade of a flowering tree, picking up the flowers that had fallen down, while Santhosh just stretched himself out. They walked back hot, tired, happy, discussing and betting on Sarala's menu for lunch.

Anupama planned to take them to the 'theatre' in the evening.

"We will go on our own, Saralakka."

Soumya and Santhosh had heard about the theatre, and they were excited. Raghunath got a driver to drive them down to the theatre and bring them back in his car. The theatre was filling up, and they ran to buy tickets. They went into the tent that it actually was and found chairs for themselves. Soumya and Anupama giggled with excitement, and Santhosh feasted on the scene around him.

"What movie is playing, by the way?" he asked.

"*Arasu*, with Puneet Rajkumar," Anupama replied.

The crowd whistled and clapped once the movie started. Watching the movie in the dark tent, with people sitting on chairs and on the floor immersed in the movie of their favourite star, was a wonderful experience. They went back home, silent and contented.

The week flew, and it was time to leave. As she left for her maternal grandmother's house in the city, Anupama realised how much Venkat had cut himself off from all that was dear to him.

***

Venkat, who had arrived that morning, was at the bus stand to pick her up. A great lunch awaited her, and she chatted about the good time she had with her friends in the village. Venkat simply smiled; he did not seem the least regretful at having missed all the fun.

Later, resting in their mother's room, Venkat told her that he had been applying abroad for a job.

"Ram uncle has promised to help me," he added.

"Which I am sure you will get." Upset as she was with this news, Anupama could not help but commend her brother. Why, he was brilliant and hardworking!

"Fingers crossed," replied her brother to that.

"But will I ever see you again, then?"

"Of course. Once I settle down, you can come and stay with me."

Anupama smiled, "For always?"

"That is up to you. I will never come back, for sure. *Ajji* and *thaatha* can visit us there." he added, referring to their grandparents.

"Well, I still have studies here," Anupama said with a faraway look and gave a small shrug.

They went onto the balcony, their favourite place, and Anupama sat on the swing. Twirling gently, she continued to talk about her trip to the village and, in between, asked him questions about his work.

***

For her eleventh and twelfth grades, Anupama had decided to take the humanities stream in the same school— not for her Physics and Mathematics that her brother excelled in! Soumya opted for science; she wanted to study Medicine and be a doctor. Senior Secondary Board exams were extremely competitive, and Anupama saw less of her friends than she would have liked to. Though not as challenging as the science stream, Anupama enjoyed humanities and worked hard to get great scores. She worked as part of the school cultural team, quietly contributing during pre-event activities and at registration during the event. She wrote well, and the team made use of her for writing the brochure and invite, and post-event release.

Sarala took care of all her needs as before. Her uniforms were washed and ironed, and her lunch was packed with delicious food that her friends loved to taste.

Soumya was busy with tuition and she sometimes came home under the pretext of doing "combined studies" for English, their only common paper. They ate, gossiped, laughed, and studied in between.

The Twelfth Board exam was nerve-wracking; both girls worked hard to excel. Soumya had the medical entrance exams to take as well, and her studies went on for some more time. Anupama applied at a few well-known arts colleges in the city and waited for the admission lists to be out. A lot was happening at home, and there was no peace. Her brother's applications abroad were being processed, and he received a good offer from a multinational IT company.

He called Anupama and gave her the news.

"I am with *ajji* and *thaatha* for a few days before I leave for California. Why don't you come?"

He refused to speak to his father when Anupama asked him to.

"No way," he said, "I know I have *amma's* blessings. That is enough. Let me know once you book your ticket; I will pick you up at the station."

Anupama gently broke the news to her father and Sarala. Her father sighed. His brother Ramnath had kept him posted, and he knew that Venkat had received a good offer. He was

Thaatha: Grandfather

happy for his son but wondered if he would ever see him again.

"How did things come to such a pass?" he asked Latha in his mind.

***

Venkat and Anupama enjoyed their break with their grandparents. Their grandmother taught Venkat the basics of cooking, and they went shopping for some utensils for him to take to the US. She packed spices and pickles too. Anupama helped in packing and kept a checklist to make sure they didn't miss out on anything important. Their grandfather had booked his tickets for him and refused to take the money from Venkat.

"Don't even think of it. Everything we have is for you both."

The day to leave arrived. Anupama and her grandparents accompanied Venkat to the airport. The airport was at the other end of the city, and they took a taxi.

***

Venkat gave her an affectionate hug, took leave from his grandparents, and walked into the airport.

"I shall call once I reach. Mail me, keep in touch," he said as he waved them goodbye.

***

The future looked lonely again for Anupama. Was her brother running away? Would she? She could not answer the questions; she did not want to. All she knew was that she would not be seeing her brother for a long, long time.

Her thoughts wandered to her school days. School was a second home, sometimes more than home. Her brother was the toast of the teachers; he was made school pupil leader in his twelfth standard. Venkat had not allowed the tragedy at home to distract him from his duties at school.

Not as outgoing or talented as her brother, Anupama had kept a low profile and withdrawn more to herself and her small group of close friends after her mother's death. Still, she knew everyone for as long as she could remember and always felt safe and loved. Anupama suddenly realised that she was not really looking forward to college— higher studies, yes, but making new friends? Her close friends had opted for different courses, and she would have to start all alone. "Oh no," she thought. Making new friends meant letting them know about family, her brother, Saralakaka… "Why did Venkat do this? I am sure *amma* is not approving of this," she thought, anguished. She knew *amma's* blessings were always with them, but to treat *appa* like this? Much as she loved her brother, she cringed as she thought of Venkat's behaviour towards their father. Mind and heart too heavy for further thought, she closed her eyes and fell asleep in the taxi on their way back home.

***

CHAPTER FOUR
College

Busy as Soumya was, it did not stop Anupama and her from going out for a movie or shopping for clothes "for college" once in a while. They pleaded with Santhosh to drive them around whenever they had big shopping plans, and he obliged sometimes.

This summer, she did not visit her father's village. Sarala went on her own to spend some time with Chinnappa.

***

Admissions were announced in various colleges and she carefully chose the college known for its Economics department. She went to the college with a few of her school friends who had applied for other courses in the same college. They had to wait in a never-ending line the entire morning to pay the fees, and by the time she was done, Anupama was tired but happy—she had got the three majors she wanted : Economics, History, and English.

Back home, sitting at the dining table, as she had her lunch, she wished she could discuss her college and prospects with her brother or mother. Lunch over, she got back to her room and emailed her brother about the college and the course. She called her grandparents and gave them the news.

Now that admissions were done, all she had to do was wait for college to open for students of the first-year degree. Her *veena* stood in the corner of her room; somehow, she did not feel like playing it; she rarely did after her father's second marriage. She bought herself a drawing record and pencils and spent time drawing; she was a good artist. She borrowed books for herself and Sarala from the lending library.

Soumya, having written her medical entrance examinations, was awaiting her results. She had passed the tests. Anupama was lazing in her room when Soumya came running in.

"Anno, I have my medical interview next week. Will you come with me?"

"But of course!"

The girls were excited and eagerly waited for the day of the interview. Soumya and her mother, Kamala auntie, picked her up in the morning, and they were on their way to the venue. Anupama's jaw dropped in amazement at the number of candidates gathered there for the interview.

"Oh wow. All the best, Soumya!"

Soumya giggled nervously, "I know! Thanks, I need it."

Soumya went in to give her attendance and waited in the line with the other candidates.

Anupama and Kamala auntie waited under the shade of a tree.

"Thanks, Auntie," Anupama said, happily taking the snacks that Soumya's mother gave her. They spent the entire morning at the venue. Soumya's mother exchanged pleasantries and notes with other mothers. Anupama spotted Soumya in the line and walked up to chat with her.

Soumya's interview was over by lunchtime, and she was hopeful.

"I did okay. I hope I impressed them."

They walked down to a nearby restaurant, had a good lunch, and took a *rickshaw* back home.

***

Anupama had to start college a week later. She and Soumya went through all her new clothes and accessories and planned what she would wear on the first day.

"This one," Soumya finally approved of a blue and white floral printed top that they had picked together on one of their outings to go with her jeans.

For the first time, Anupama entered the classroom alone. Soumya and she always went to school together, and she hated being alone in a new place. She walked in, trying to be as inconspicuous as possible, and quietly took a seat in the second row.

But by the end of the day, she was hopeful and happy; her classes were great.

***

Soumya got admission to the government medical college in Bangalore. Her father, a government officer, took a transfer so that they could move with her. Everything happened quickly. Anupama and Soumya were inconsolable at the thought of not being together anymore. Sarala and Soumya's mother were teary-eyed as they wished each other goodbye. The girls hugged each other and cried.

Rickshaw. A three-wheeled 'cab' popular in India

"Text me and call whenever you're free," said Anupama. Both girls had just been gifted a cell phone each by their respective dads. "I shall do so, too," she promised.

Soumya's mother gave her a fond hug. "Do well, sweetheart. God bless," she said to her as she got into the car.

The men spoke in soft tones and bid each other goodbye.

"Call me when you want to go shopping. I will take you around!" joked Santhosh. He had joined his college hostel in Mysore, having one more year to go before graduation.

The girls laughed through their tears at this, and soon Anupama was waving goodbye to her much-loved neighbours, who were family to her through all her sorrows and joys.

***

Venkat called her that night. Suddenly, he felt guilty for having left his sister to deal with life on her own.

"Do come when you have your summer holidays. I also want you to meet someone here," he confided.

Anupama was excited to hear about the 'someone', but her brother only said,

"Come here and meet her!"

Slowly, Anupama had her own group of friends in college, with whom she did not mind sharing that the one who packed her tasty lunches was "...not her mother, but Saralakka, who her father married after her mother died." Her brother, she told them, worked in the US, not willing to give any more details.

Her loneliness at home only increased now that she did not have Soumya's house to escape to.

Soumya and she texted each other regularly; the calls got rarer as they both got busy with studies.

Sarala in her quiet way tried to keep Anupama occupied at home when she was not studying or reading. "Help me with laying the table for dinner?" she peeped into her room one night. "I am not feeling too good."

Anupama jumped out of bed on which she was stretched out, idly going through her phone, suddenly feeling guilty. She was always preoccupied with herself!

"Sure, Saralakka," she said as she put her phone down and walked to the kitchen.

Slowly, without realising it, Anupama started to assist Sarala in the kitchen, and Sarala took the opportunity to teach her some basics of cooking. Anupama helped in grinding chutneys and masalas, and now packed her lunch for college herself.

She helped her make rice snacks, grinding old cooked rice to paste, mixing the salt and spices in, shaping them, and spreading them out to dry on the terrace, making sure they were covered with nylon nets so that birds did not steal them. She learned to draw the *rangoli* in the courtyard; she enjoyed it. Sarala knew so many designs! Anupama felt a new respect for her; why, she cooked so well, and she knew so much! They went together to the library and discussed books as they surfed through them on the shelves. Raghunath watched with relief the slow re-bonding between his daughter and her new mother. She continued to address her as Saralakka, though. He sighed. Well, this was more than he hoped for!

In college, though, she kept her personal life strictly private and did not chat about 'dad' and 'mom' like her friends did. She missed Soumya and Kamala auntie, with whom she could share anything.

***

Her favourite subject was definitely Economics. They had a new teacher in her third year, and he was "amazing," as the students exclaimed after his first class. Murali sir, as they called him, was just the teacher and mentor Anupama was looking for. During their mentorship sessions, she tried to learn as much as she could from him.

She worked hard, as was her nature to do so, and graduated with excellent scores. She stood third in her university, much to the pride of her teachers and father. For the graduation day ceremony, she had to wear formals— white saree— as per university rules. Sarala offered to take her shopping, but Anupama decided to check her mother's almirah once. Yes, she remembered right! Her mother's beautiful white and red Bengali cotton saree was neatly dry cleaned and kept along with the others; it was still very wearable. Sarala and she went out shopping for matching blouse material, and gave it to the tailor for stitching.

The Graduation Day was an emotional day for her and Raghunath; they missed her mother. But Anupama felt a happiness too, wearing her mother's saree, she felt she was wrapped in her mother's loving arms. Soumya had taken a day's leave and attended the Graduation Day with Santhosh. Santhosh had completed his engineering a year earlier and was preparing to take the civil services exams that year.

Venki called her and congratulated her on her rank and medals, and she emailed him photos of the ceremony.

***

She had long holidays and travelled to Bangalore to spend time with her grandparents once she had sent in applications for postgraduate courses in Economics and Literature. She and Soumya visited each other during the weekends. Anupama enjoyed the warmth and comfort of being with her grandparents and helped her grandmother with cooking. She took her grandmother out for movies, and they enjoyed their outings together. To her grandparents, it was like reliving the past with the daughter they lost.

Venki called and suggested she apply at universities in the US She was not sure; she preferred to do her Masters in Mysore and "…probably think about it later," she told him.

***

She joined the university to do her Masters in Economics. Postgraduation was fun, and she enjoyed the challenging assignments and projects. She and her classmate Richa wrote research papers and presented them at seminars. She felt brighter and happier than she had ever felt before.

For her three-month internship during the last term, she applied to be part of a socio-economic project at a premier central institute in Bangalore. Apart from the project, Bangalore had its attractions— living in her grandparents' home, and visiting Soumya and her family. Santhosh had passed the civil services examination and was away on training.

***

Two years flew by. After her Masters, which she cleared with great scores, she expressed her desire to do her PhD in Economics. Raghunath was not too keen.

"Maybe it is time to look for a groom?" he asked.

Anupama shook her head vehemently. "Of course not, *Appa*. There is so much that I want to do. *Amma* always told us that she wanted us to be highly educated! I have already taken the qualifying examination and hope to pass it. And I want to be financially independent, too. How can you even think of getting me married now, *Appa*?"

Sarala supported Anupama's decision, too.

Anupama approached Murali sir to be her guide, and he agreed. She registered herself as a research fellow at the university. Murali sir and she thrashed out topic ideas. Villages were close to Anupama's heart. Nearly every summer of her younger life was spent in her father's ancestral house in the village. The closeness she shared with her grandmother, the yearly trips with her mother, father and brother, the relatives in the village who poured in to meet them, her later trips with Sarala and her father, her trips to Sarala's house, the river, the fresh milk and food— they were all dear to her, part of the fond memories she had. She had not consciously realised this until she decided on her postgraduate studies in Economics, and when she registered for her PhD, she had no doubt that it had to do with villages.

The rural Indian was at the focus of marketing, with the capacity of the rural household for consumption having gone up, according to surveys and magazines. Of course, a study on the various rural marketing strategies with a focus on the rural consumer's buying behaviour would definitely be relevant, she decided. Her guide supported her decision and she was set.

It was not all research, though. Being a full-time scholar, Anupama was expected to give lectures and assist in administrative work at the department.

Anupama prepared meticulously for the survey. She drew an elaborate flow chart. She finalised the district to be studied and used a scientific method to select the villages.

She wished she could ask Sarala to join her and help with fieldwork. It was not to be, though. She could not bring herself to ask her; she would not. She had not grown close enough to her for that. Raghunath suggested that Sarala accompany her to the villages. Anupama did not respond. She asked her guide if he knew anyone who could accompany her.

"Ask Pooja," Murali sir advised her. "She has a rural-based topic for her dissertation. This will be a good exposure for her."

Pooja, an MPhil student in the department, was more than happy to assist her in fieldwork. Anupama gave them some class lectures, and Pooja had high regard for her.

***

CHAPTER FIVE

The Village

Field work was a whole new experience. Comfortable as she was in the rural milieu, each encounter brought a surprise. The first village was about two hours from the city. Pooja and she left for the bus terminus early in the morning and were amazed to see the crowd. They had to stand in a long queue for the tickets and were stumped by the frantic crowd jostling to get a seat on the bus. They found themselves being pushed into the bus and found a seat, wide-eyed at the experience.

"Whew," Anupama breathed out. "Welcome to PhD!"

It soon turned out to be fun. It being a Saturday, children were out playing in the streets. They followed her and Pooja around the village. Some houses had no numbers! Anupama had to ditch her carefully listed samples and select her houses systematically. She selected every fourth/fifth house in every second road, depending on the number of questionnaires she wanted filled in that village. Some women came running hearing about the survey, "So what do we get in return?"

"No, no," said a slightly embarrassed Anupama, "this is for my degree."

"We give the answers, and you get your degree!" they commented when they realised that there were no gifts or money being given.

Tired, but satisfied at the end of the day, Anupama and Pooja headed back to the city. This time they made sure they were not pushed and elbowed as they climbed the bus; Pooja got in quickly and saved the seat next to hers for Anupama.

The next village was not very far away, too. Only when they got off the bus did they realise that the village on their list was a two-kilometre walk from the bus stop. They walked down slowly, luckily it was December and the sun was weak. When she finally started her survey, people smiled when she wanted to know what toilet soaps they used. "Did you notice the ponds as you walked down the road to our village? Well, we use the red mud there for a bath!"

They laughed at the look on Anupama and Pooja's faces. "It is as good as any soap," they swore.

In most villages, people used the "red carbolic soap" that the village doctor recommended for the children, or the pink soap that "smelled of roses". An educated young mother swore by the "baby soap" that she got for her child from the nearest town.

The last few villages were far, almost bordering the neighbouring state. Raghunath's cousin Sivappa, a small farmer, lived in one of the villages with his family of mother, wife, and daughter. Raghunath informed him of Anupama's visit.

The simple family was delighted to have two visitors from the city. Anupama was used to a village and life there, but for Pooja, this was her first stay in a village, and she was excited.

Sivappa met them at the bus stand, and they walked home. His wife had made a simple lunch of rice and lentil curry, with a beautifully made egg omelette for each of them. They went for field work in the nearby village after lunch. Sivappa introduced them to the first house they went to.

"Aren't you getting married? You are old enough to have a child," commented an old woman in the house cheekily.

"*She* looks young," she continued, pointing at Pooja.

Anupama and Pooja exchanged grins. "Good beginning," whispered Anupama as she turned to the old woman, "*Ajji*, I am only 24! Why do you want me married off so soon?"

"24! I had three children at your age," commented the old woman, shaking her head.

It angered the two of them to see thatched huts overflowing with children. "How can you afford to have so many children?" Anupama questioned. "What logic is there in having so many?"

And it upset them when, even in the poorest households, they wanted to know their caste before deciding to answer her questionnaire or welcome them to a meal or a cool drink of buttermilk.

"No, Pooja, leave it," Anupama advised when the younger girl was about to retort angrily at one such question.

"My daughter is inside," an old, poor woman said, pointing at her hut.

"Can I go in and ask her some questions, *Amma*?"

The old woman looked at her and asked, "Which community are you from?"

It was exasperating. But Anupama answered casually, "Why, I belong to your community, of course!" That was the majority community in that village. She knew and hoped the woman was one of them, too.

Once inside, she saw the daughter— a newborn baby was sleeping peacefully next to his young mother inside the small dark hut. Moved at the sight, she pressed some money into the sleeping child's palm and walked out, strangely emotional.

It was about 4 p.m. by the time they were done with the survey in the village. The sunny day suddenly grew dark and sombre, and they quickly walked to the bus stop.

"The last bus has left," the elderly men sitting under the tree told them. "You need to walk to the next bus stop near the town."

"That's a good two kilometres away," Sivappa told Anupama and Pooja.

The village was bordering the Karnataka and Kerala forests on one side, and Anupama and Pooja were startled to hear noises coming from the forest.

"Those are elephants. You'd better leave!"

"Sivappa, let's go!" Anupama and Pooja spoke urgently.

They thanked the men and started walking down the narrow mud path in the forest, towards the nearest bus stop in the town.

Anupama sensed something behind her—both she and Pooja looked back instinctively and were amazed to see dark clouds following them.

"Sivappa, we are being followed by dark clouds! And we are being chased by the rain!" They shouted with excitement as they picked up pace and ran. They couldn't beat the clouds, though; the rains soon caught up with them, and they were drenched to the bone by the time they reached the bus stop and took shelter under the front awning of a tea shop.

Shivering, they sipped hot tea as they waited for the bus. It was an experience Anupama would never forget.

***

Karihalli was a three-kilometre walk from the nearest bus stop, which was at the village of Madenahalli. Anupama and Pooja took an early bus and reached Madenahalli by eight in the morning. As they walked into Madenahalli towards Karihalli, Anupama noticed with satisfaction the prosperity of the village. It was a chilly December morning, and the roads were strewn with groundnuts, spread out to dry. The fields were lush with growing sugarcane —they would be ready in time for the harvest festival in January. The canals had clean, clear water flowing in the fields. She was transported back to her father's village: her grandmother's house, which was always full of milk, fruits— especially mangoes, and food grains; the river, the fields and of course Sarala's house— the old shack at the edge of the rice fields had been brought down to build a new concrete building after the marriage.

"Isn't this really nice?" Pooja was saying. Some of the girls in the village approached them curiously. "Please come home and have some milk," one of the older ones said. When Anupama thanked her but refused, saying they had a lot to do, the girls gave them a fistful of groundnuts.

"How much further to Karihalli?" Anupama asked.

"Karihalli? Why would anyone want to go there?" the girls asked.

Anupama explained patiently.

"What is the use of asking anyone in that village? Ask us the questions here!"

When Anupama again patiently explained that Karihalli was in her selection of villages, the eldest one shrugged, "It is another half a kilometre from here. In fact, you don't have to come back through our village once you finish your work. Take the other route; you will come to a bus stop on the highway."

Anupama was curious, but thought it better than to discuss the village.

***

The road leading to the village became deserted as they reached the outskirts of Madenahalli. Anupama noticed crude fences at certain stretches, as if someone was trying to form a boundary.

Karihalli was a small brown village, with small huts and narrow mud roads. Old women and men lay down in the verandah where there were patches of sunlight. A group of curious children followed them. Anupama's attention was on the houses. There were no proper door numbers here, so she had to choose the houses she would visit to fill out her questionnaire.

"Is your mother at home?" she asked the girl who was standing on her verandah and watching her.

The girl ran in to call her mother. The woman was in her thirties, and if her answers were any indication, there was not much one could say about the village.

The men had already gone to the fields, and they had to wait until early evening to talk to them.

As they moved around, the children followed them, curious and excited, asking questions, giggling, and eager to help. They were mostly thin and grubby; the slightly older ones carried the younger ones. It was Christmas holiday time, so they were not in school. Something seemed to be troubling the older ones, though.

Finally, the oldest of them, a boy of about 12, asked,

"How come you have entered our village?"

"What do you mean?" asked Anupama, startled at the unexpected question.

"Nobody really comes here. We are not even allowed to enter Madenahalli, except for working in the fields. So, how come?"

"I told you, I am here to do work for my studies. Why shouldn't I come here?" she asked.

"We are all *Harijans* here," the boy said, looking at her questioningly.

"So what?"

"Well, no one ever comes here," said the boy. "Except during elections." The children giggled at the memory of politicians coming to their homes for votes during last year's Election. "And of course, the school teacher."

"See," said Anupama.

"But that is about it!"

"Where is your school?" she asked, and followed the children who led the way towards the back of the village, towards Madenahalli.

Anupama noticed with curiosity the dried lake as they walked back. There were overgrown weeds, garbage, and dirt strewn all around it. "How is this possible?" she wondered.

The school was a small concrete house. The kids ran around it with excitement. Anupama and Pooja sat on the cool verandah and relaxed.

When the men came, she asked,

"What happened here?"

The older ones shrugged.

"The lake dried."

"I can see that. But why?"

"All the garbage of Madenahalli is dumped there," one of them said matter-of-factly.

"I don't understand," she shook her head. "Why do you let that happen?"

"What do you think we can do? There is nothing we can do," one of them shrugged.

Anupama was thoughtful but did not prod further.

It was evening when Anupama and Pooja walked down the village in the opposite direction of Madenahalli towards the bus stop. On the way out of the village, Anupama decided to administer the questionnaire in one last house. She craned her neck and looked over the rough fence into the house. A woman was busy cleaning vessels in the backyard, and when Anupama asked her if she could come in and ask her some questions, she replied without looking up, "Please go away.

Harijans: Meaning "people of God," to refer to the lowest caste (religious stratification) of Hindus in India, commonly known as untouchables, now a part of the Scheduled Castes

What is there for me to say? There is no water, no crops, what can I grow here? Where is the money to buy anything?"

Anupama apologised and walked away quickly.

***

20 villages and 800 rural respondents later, Anupama was ready to do her analysis and write her report.

Anupama worked hard on her analysis and writing. It was like working on her Board exams again! She worked on her computer endlessly, doing the statistics, checking out more studies for her review, and keying in the chapters. Sarala made sure she had enough to eat and filled her lunch box with food that Anupama loved so that the box would come back empty.

In eight months, she submitted the thesis. It was exhilarating! She had never felt so happy and free before. She, Pooja, and a few other research students planned to celebrate the next day.

When her father came home, she ran to him saying, "I submitted my thesis, *Appa*." She continued, "And Ram sir has assured me he will take me into the department as a permanent faculty!"

Her father patted her affectionately. "That calls for a celebration."

"Saralakka has made *payasam*!"

***

Payasam: A sweet Indian porridge-like dessert

CHAPTER SIX

The New Arrival

Sarala was awash with a wave of embarrassment, mixed with wonder. She was pregnant. Her world suddenly brightened, and it showed on her face. Raghunath broke the news gently to Anupama.

"Sarala is expecting to be a mother," he said.

Anupama was not sure she had heard it right. Sitting up on her bed, she was reading a book. She looked up and said, "Sorry, come again?"

"Sarala is pregnant, Anno," Raghunath repeated gently.

"What are you saying, *Appa*? I am 25!"

Later, when they were together, Sarala asked Raghunath if they should go ahead with the pregnancy.

"I can understand what Anupama is going through."

"This is your life, Sarala. Don't you want the child?"

"I did not dare dream about such a blessing in my life. In fact, I did not even dream of marrying again."

"Don't even talk about not having the child. It is ours," said Raghunath.

***

There was no change in Anupama's demeanour towards her father and Sarala, and it came as a shock to them when she announced one day at the dinner table, "I have been offered a research job at the university in Shimoga, and I have agreed to take it."

"But you were offered a permanent post here," said Raghunath.

"Hmm, yes. But this is an exciting research project. I thought it would be a good exposure for me too. It is a one-year project, a tie-up with a Swedish research group, and I am being paid a great sum. Moreover, I am given university accommodation, so that is no problem. I have also handed in my resignation at the college."

Raghunath had nothing to say to this. Anupama was leaving at the end of the month.

Anupama's grandparents were happy to hear that Sarala was in the family way. Anupama wondered if she should inform Venkat. She decided that this news should reach him first from her.

That night, she told him over the WhatsApp call about the pregnancy. There was silence on the other side for some time. "Who cares?" he finally said. "I have nothing to do with them anyway."

Anupama did not respond to this. She did expect such a reply, after all.

"How is Eva?" Eva was the girlfriend she was yet to meet. She had seen plenty of her pics on WhatsApp, though.

"Good. Why don't you come here?"

Anupama told him about her project at Kuvempu University in Shimoga.

"Well, take care, all the best."

Soumya called her to inform her that she had got admission as a fellow at a medical institution in the US to do her Masters. She would be joining in six months.

"I am free now, shall come and visit you," Anupama said.

She took the morning bus two days later, a Friday, and reached Soumya's house by lunchtime. Soumya's mother greeted her affectionately. Soumya got back from the hospital at teatime. She had taken off on Saturday so she could spend time with Anupama.

Anupama told her of Saralakka's pregnancy and of her own project appointment at Shimoga. Soumya realised that the news of a new addition to the family had unnerved her a little, but she did not dwell on it in their conversations— she thought it best Anupama worked it out herself.

***

Anupama was part of an exciting project funded by a Swedish development agency in Stockholm, which planned to study the economics of rural Shimoga, with a focus on self-employment opportunities for women. The agency tied up with the university, which was to provide them with an office and human resources. Anupama got in touch with Suma, a research scholar from the Department of Economics at the university, who coordinated the whole project.

Suma was enthusiastic and eager to meet her.

"You will be staying at the researcher's hostel where I stay. In fact, I have booked the room next to mine. You have an attached bath too, so you should be comfortable here."

She promised to meet her at the station to pick her up.

A bit of shopping for the things she needed for hostel life and Anupama was set. Sarala packed pickles and some dry sweets that would last her a few weeks. Anupama decided to travel alone and she dissuaded her father from travelling with her.

"Suma will pick me up at the station, *Appa*. I am reaching Shimoga in the morning; it shouldn't be a problem at all."

She booked a one-way ticket online for herself.

***

The train entered Shimoga in the morning. Anupama was already up and ready. She got off the train with her luggage and called Suma's number. Suma was waiting for her at the main entrance. Into the second year of her PhD programme, Suma was a research fellow on a monthly scholarship. A postgraduate in Economics from the university, she spent her college years in hostels, her parents being in Dubai. She was a bright, happy girl, and she was familiar with Shimoga. She drove round in her Maruti Zen, which she had had for ages. "Wouldn't think of giving it away," she always said.

They greeted each other cheerfully.

"Here, let me keep your luggage in the boot, ma'am."

"Call me Anupama, Suma."

"Ok, Anupama ma'am." They both laughed.

Once in the car, Anupama sent a 'reached safely' message to her father.

Suma spoke all the way to the hostel, identifying the places they passed on the way. By the time they reached the university,

Anupama was hungry. They walked up to the warden's room and introductions done, Suma collected the key to Anupama's room, and they lugged the suitcases up to the first floor where her room was. Having grown up in the private and protective environment of her home, Anupama suddenly felt strange in the empty hall, with one or two students lounging in the reception reading newspapers. Most doors were shut, and she saw small, cluttered rooms when she peeped into an occasional open door. Each room was shared by two students; only researchers and staff like her were given single rooms.

They reached her room, and Suma unlocked the door. In they went into a tiny room, mercifully bright, and when the windows were opened, airy. The window looked into the hostel garden, and Anupama was thankful for the privacy.

"Freshen up, and we will go for breakfast," Suma said cheerfully. "I will be back in 20 minutes."

Anupama shut the door behind her and flopped down on the bed, hands stretched out, looking up at the whirring ceiling fan.

"What am I doing?" she thought, overwhelmed by the silent and empty hostel. "Am I running away?"

She sat up suddenly. Was she running away? Like her brother did? She couldn't believe it. What about *appa*? How did she do this?

She called her father. "Hello, *Appa*. I have reached the hostel. Yes, the room is nice. Yes, Suma is nice, too. Yes, I am going to have breakfast once I freshen up." She answered the questions shot at her by her concerned and relieved father. She hesitated, for a second only, "Say hi to Saralakka for me. Bye."

Feeling better, she showered, dressed, and knocked at Suma's door, hungry and ready for breakfast. Breakfast was not bad; it was not a patch on Saralakka's cooking, but not being a fussy eater, she enjoyed it, and they headed for the department.

***

There was a lot to do, and Anupama was happy. She met Professor Ananthakrishna, whose project it was that she was working for. The Swedish project staff were yet to arrive; they were expected only the next week.

Without much ado, the professor briefed her about her work for the project. She and Suma went through the project proposal and familiarised themselves with the project, the places, and people they were supposed to meet, survey and interview for their project. They started work on the questionnaires and data forms with the help of the professor.

The students had a small break between their semesters, and Suma was rather free. She spent most of her time with Anupama, and they worked together.

A week later, they drove down to the station to receive Liam Johansson and Freja Svensson, the Swedish researchers.

"So, when are you going home for a vacation?" Anupama asked as they drove down to the station.

Suma shrugged. "Depends on when one of them will want me to."

Anupama looked at her puzzled.

"Well, mom has her own family and dad has his own. I grew up in hostels in India," she said matter-of-factly. "No complaints. I enjoy my freedom."

Anupama did not reply. She did not know what to say. This was a situation she had not encountered.

"Grandparents?" She finally asked.

Suma shrugged again. "Mom's parents are in Bangalore. I go there sometimes."

Somehow, this made Anupama feel better. Her mother's parents' house in Bangalore was her most favourite place in the world, and she was happy that Suma had one such haven, too.

"They are nice."

"Mine are nice too." Anupama smiled.

***

Liam Johansson and Freja Svensson were young researchers about Anupama's age, excited to be in India; this was their first project abroad. They had a long journey, landing in Mumbai, then a flight to Bangalore, and then the train to Shimoga.

Introductions done, Suma put them in a taxi—her car was too small to fit them and their luggage—and drove ahead of them.

The girls were equally excited to meet the foreign researchers and were raring to go ahead with the project.

Their rooms were in the same building as those of Anupama and Suma, and on the same floor.

"Shall meet you both down in 20 minutes," Suma told them cheerfully.

And sure enough, the hungry duo was ready, and they were all walking to the canteen in 20 minutes. With still an hour's time to go for the professor to come to the department, the Swedes went back to their rooms to rest and unpack.

Suma called them from the department when Professor Ananthakrishna came in.

Soon, all were deep in work, reworking the questionnaires, planning the villages to visit, and getting contacts in each of the places.

The four of them worked well together, and time flew. The field visits to meet rural women were to begin in two months.

***

In the evenings, the foursome spent time together discovering the city and its various small restaurants serving delicious food. Of course, it was always in Suma's old Maruti Zen. They went to the Tunga river and sat on the bank, just watching the water flow.

"The Cauvery flows in my dad's village," Anupama found herself saying one day. She had not spoken of her home or family before. "We used to go there every summer. It was great."

"So, you might miss it this summer."

"Haven't been there in a long time, actually, since my undergrad days, come to think of it."

"Oh well, it is not like you may never go there again!" smiled Liam, the optimistic one in the group.

Anupama shrugged lightly and lapsed into silence, as if she regretted saying anything at all.

They sat there together, comfortable in the silence, until twilight fell. They got up, drove around the neighbourhood until they found a nice restaurant to eat in, and got back to the hostel after a good meal.

***

Anupama, Liam, and Freja worked hard in the department, getting the project details ready. Classes for the next semester began, and Suma was busy giving lectures and working on her own research. She made it a point to meet them in their office every day, though, and the evenings were always spent together. Anupama was comfortable in their company, though she did not really open up about her family, and none of them bothered her about home and family.

This being their first project outside Sweden, Liam and Freja missed home, but for a short time only. Their work, the warmth of the people around, the friendly greetings of students whom they met in the department in the mornings, Suma and Anupama's company, soon made them feel comfortable. Both were cheerful and accepted things as they saw them; they did not fuss about anything, including the weather, and enjoyed Indian food.

***

They were three months into the project when she got a call from Murali sir that her public viva voce was scheduled for the next week, and she dashed home for a day. Her viva went off well, and she was declared a PhD degree holder.

***

Suma insisted on accompanying them on fieldwork, and Liam agreed provided she let them pay for it. They planned to complete it before the rains came so they could stay indoors and do the analysis and writing during the monsoon.

It was with a feeling of *déjà vu* that Anupama got into the crowded, rickety mofussil bus with the others. They found a place in the last row and occupied it, and soon realised why it was empty. They were jostled up and down and tossed sideways as the bus picked up speed— they giggled hysterically as they desperately hung on tight to the handlebars of the seat in front of them.

They got off at their destination, a little shaky, and took some time to regain their breath before they started off to the village administrative office. They met Boranna who was waiting for them, having been informed by Professor Ananthakrishna. He was to be their guide and companion and had already arranged for them to meet the women of the village at the small community hall.

The hall was bright and noisy. Women sat talking, waiting for them, and children ran around playing. The session went on well, and soon it was lunchtime. Boranna had also arranged for their lunch— his wife brought them food that she had cooked, packed in boxes, and they had a simple and lovely meal of rice, dhal, and vegetables.

It was after one such trip, on their way back to the campus, that Anupama finally opened up.

"Wasn't lunch great!" she sighed with satisfaction. "Only Saralakka can beat that kind of cooking."

"Who is Saralakka?"

"Dad's wife."

"My stepmom," she hastened to add, at the look on Suma's face.

"And your mom?" asked Suma.

"She passed away when I was eight."

There was a sympathetic silence at this.

"I am well, though. Saralakka is nice."

"Well, that's great, then," laughed Liam.

"So why the silence about home?" the discerning Freja asked.

Anupama did not answer for a while. "I don't know," she shrugged. "My brother disowned my dad and went away once the marriage happened."

"Well, I have had two stepmoms," laughed Freja.

"But you have mom, too, right?" replied Anupama. "I am okay, as I said. But now, Saralakka is having a baby! I am 25!"

There was silence. Suma did not know what to say. She was a non-judgemental person, having grown up the hard way on her own. She had affectionate parents and loved them in return. She also had much younger siblings on both sides.

"My dad's son is joining school this summer," she said.

No one spoke for some time. They knew it was a big deal for Anupama that she even confided in them. Anupama was quiet, deep in thought. She seemed to have developed a mental block; she could not accept that there was another child coming into the family, that too when she was so much older! Was her heart not big enough to welcome one more human into her life? She did not know, and at that time, did not want to think about it.

***

Her dad called her one day, as she was on yet another bus travelling to yet another village, to inform her that Sarala had given birth to a baby girl, and that both were safe. He sounded happy.

"That's good," Anupama replied. "I am on a bus right now, *Appa*, shall call you later."

***

Again, fieldwork was an enriching experience; the native wisdom of rural folk and attitude towards life never failed to amaze Anupama. Fieldwork done, they sat for long hours together and worked on the data while it poured outside. Anupama was invited to give some lectures to the final-year students, and she did so readily. As the project was nearing completion, Freja persuaded Anupama to apply to their agency in Sweden for funding for a rural project.

With nothing planned for the immediate future, Anupama agreed and, with Suma, prepared a budget proposal for a rural project and sent it for approval.

***

Venkat called her that Sunday morning, as he did every weekend.

"How much longer?" he asked.

"Another three months to go," she replied.

She knew what was coming.

"Apply for a tourist visa to the US. I will book your tickets for you."

Having nothing else planned, she agreed. She could probably visit Soumya there as well, Anupama thought, having been too busy with field work to see Soumya off when she left for the US to do her Masters.

She did not want to go back home. She took a weekend off and travelled to her grandparents' home from where she got her visa applications going.

Her grandmother gently tried to convince her to go home.

She showed her pictures of the newborn, which she had taken on her phone, when they went to visit the mother and child.

"Not now, *Ajji*. I need some time," Anupama gently but firmly avoided the topic.

***

The report was done and submitted, and Professor Ananthakrishna was satisfied with their work.

Suma and Anupama dropped Liam and Freja at the station. The Swedes parted with hugs and promises to keep in touch as they bid them goodbye.

Anupama was leaving in two days' time for her grandparents' home. She was flying to the US from there in two weeks. Having earned a great sum from the project and not having had avenues to spend it, she had saved a lot of money and did not have to depend on Venkat for her finances. Besides, he had already booked her tickets for her.

She gently refused when Raghunath asked her to come home and spend time with them.

Her grandparents, happy to have her with them, were nevertheless upset with her decision.

"Running away like Venkat, are we?" asked her grandfather that night as they sat together watching TV after dinner.

"I am not proud of what I am doing," Anupama admitted. "I don't know why I am doing this. But I am not running away, *Thaatha*. I will be back in two months, if not earlier."

"And then what?"

"Let me think of that later."

Inside, she felt small and narrow-minded, but she wanted to do this for herself.

***

CHAPTER SEVEN

The Decision

Raghunath came to her grandparents' home to spend some time with Anupama. It had been a year since she saw him, except for the brief visit she paid them to attend her viva, and Anupama had not wanted him to visit her at Shimoga. He was also busy with Sarala's pregnancy and childbirth. Now that their maid had agreed to stay full-time to help take care of Sarala, and Chinnappa was at home, he came over to spend time with his daughter.

Anupama was happy to see him. It had indeed been a long time since she saw her father; never had she been away from him for so long. He brought her favourite coconut *burfi* and *rava laddoos*, specially made for her by Sarala.

She enjoyed the sweets. "Thank Saralakka for me, *Appa*, these are delicious." she said.

They sat together and spoke for a long time, with her grandparents joining in. Anupama was happy and contented, something she hadn't felt in a long time. Not once did she enquire about the baby; she couldn't help it, she was simply not interested.

Coconut burfi and rava laddoos: Indian sweets

Raghunath stayed on for a week, and left for home after accompanying Anupama to the airport to see her off.

***

It was a long, tiring journey. She had to change flights in Frankfurt. Her brother had given her clear instructions on the entire procedure, and she had little trouble at the layovers.

Venkat was at the San Jose airport to receive her. Seeing her brother after so many years made her emotional, and she hugged him happily. As he drove her to his apartment, Venkat broke the news, "Eva and I are getting married this Sunday. *Ajji* and *thaatha* know. I told them I wanted it to be a surprise for you."

"So of course, even *appa* knows."

He shrugged. "Ram uncle and auntie are flying down from San Francisco tomorrow."

"Wow, that's great. No wonder," she laughed, "*Ajji* persuaded me to pack a silk saree!"

He asked her about her project in Shimoga. She was still chatting about her project experience. Suma, Liam, and Freja as they drove into the apartment complex.

"Wow, this is beautiful." she said, looking around her.

Her brother's flat was huge, and her room was lovely. She lay on the bed and was soon fast asleep.

***

She met Eva that evening. Anupama found her pleasant and attractive, and she saw that her brother was clearly happy in her company.

When she left after dinner, Anupama asked, "Does she know that you are not in touch with *appa*?"

"She does. She wants me to invite him to the wedding."

"Why didn't you, then?" asked Anupama.

Venkat just shrugged.

Later in the night, she spoke to her father, "I met Eva, Venkat's fiancé. She is nice, *Appa*. It seems she wanted you to be invited for the wedding."

"She did, she got my number from Ram and has sent me an invite on WhatsApp. She says she hopes to meet me soon." Raghunath sounded optimistic, and Anupama was happy for him.

Her uncle and aunt reached the next day, and Anupama was busy going out, shopping, and inviting Indian friends of theirs who lived in San Jose. She was thankful she had packed her silks—she chose to wear one of them instead of buying a new one for herself.

She had brought plenty of dry sweets and savouries that her grandmother made for Venkat, and he was thrilled to get them.

They had a simple church wedding. Both Venkat and Eva worked in the same company, and a whole lot of friends and colleagues were present. Lunch was delicious.

Anupama left with her uncle and aunt after the wedding. She bid her brother a tearful goodbye; she would not be coming back to San Jose. Anupama was planning to travel across America from San Francisco— Soumya had her semester break — and she was going to Chicago to spend two weeks with her. She had booked a ticket by bus from

San Francisco; she wanted to travel by road, and Venkat had booked her return ticket to India from Chicago. She did not want to stay back in the US for longer; she was not used to having so much free time. She was already restless and wanted to get back to work.

San Francisco was fun. A childless couple, her uncle and aunt doted on Anupama and Venkat. They were happy and excited that Anupama was spending a fortnight with them. She spent most of her days walking around the city and visiting its famous landmarks. People from different cultures blended and worked and lived in the city. Anupama, restricted by the personal troubles in her life, opened up and enjoyed her trips across the city. Her uncle and aunt were always there for her after work, and evenings were spent together, lazing at home, with an occasional dinner out. Her aunt shopped for the newborn and gave her a bag full of frocks and gifts for the child. Anupama was not too keen and considered it extra baggage. She herself bought two shirts for her father, some coral beads for Saralakka, some nuts and chocolates for her grandparents, and a few tops for Suma, who was coming to her grandparents' house to meet her.

***

She bade an affectionate goodbye to her uncle and aunt and boarded the bus to Chicago city.

There were lots of stops in between during the two-day and 6 to 7 hour drive, and she was excited. It was fall, and it got more beautiful and colder as she headed east. She mostly looked out of her window into the view outside; at other times, she slept, read, listened to music on her headphones, or chatted with her neighbour on the bus. She got off at all the stops just to feel the place and stretch out. At longer stops, she freshened up at the restrooms and bought some curios as souvenirs for herself.

Her neighbour on the bus was a college freshman studying in Chicago. He was curious about India, its population, economy, and its democratic form of government. He was particularly interested in her research work.

As she chatted with him and answered his questions, the image of Karihalli and the woman who shooed her off flashed in her mind. It made her uncomfortable; she could not say why.

***

Tired, happy, and eager to meet Soumya, she finally got off at the Illinois Union Station late in the evening, two days after she left San Francisco. She bid a cheerful goodbye to her freshman friend and the driver of the bus.

Soumya was there waiting for her, and they hugged each other with joy. They got into Soumya's car and chatted all the way to her tiny apartment.

"Am I glad you planned your trip when you did! It is going to be so much fun!"

And it was fun. The two of them enjoyed themselves going around the city. They walked each day in a new direction so as to see as much of the city as possible.

***

They were making breakfast one morning when Soumya told her about Mohit, her colleague and fellow student. "We hit it off immediately. I know it is too early to say anything, but I can see myself spending the rest of my life with him. I think he likes me, too."

"Ooh, big words! The eternal romantic, Soumya," Anupama laughed, "Seriously, I am thrilled for you. When do I get to meet him?"

"He has invited us and a few other friends for dinner tonight."

"Uh oh. Do we have to?"

***

Most of them had already heard of her; they were also friends of Soumya's. She had a good time and liked Mohit, handsome, unassuming, and brilliant. It was obvious that Soumya was special to him too.

As they drove back after dinner, Soumya asked her if she had not met anyone interesting so far.

"With all the baggage I am carrying, I am in no mood for a relationship," Anupama shrugged.

"It is not a baggage that you have to carry! Look at Venkat. Why are you carrying his baggage also, by the way? It is not baggage, it is garbage, dump it in a dustbin and live your life."

When Anupama did not reply, Soumya glanced at her shrewdly.

"I know why you are upset about the baby."

"Me, upset? How do you know?"

"I am your best friend. So, what if you, at this age, have a new sibling? It is Saralakka's life, and her first child. You wouldn't grudge her happiness, Anno. I know you too well to think that. Venkat couldn't bear to share Raghu uncle and you with Saralakka, and you cannot bear to share Saralakka with the little one. Right?"

Anupama was stunned. Was this the reason why she was running away? She shook her head slowly.

"No, Soumya. It is not that. Honestly."

They lapsed into silence, each in their own world of thoughts.

Was Soumya right? No, it was not that she was unwilling to share Saralakka with one more person. Realisation poured down on her like a sudden shower of rain on a hot morning: unexpected, discomforting, but nevertheless welcome. Welcome? She was not sure; she felt stupid!

She was jealous, that was it! She had lost her mother, now she couldn't think of losing Saralakka to another person. It was not about her not wanting to share Saralakka, it was about whether Saralakka would continue to care for her like she did, now that she had a child of her own! Her ego was trying to find a balance; she was trying to be detached; she was actually not ignoring the child and Saralakka. It had made her so happy to see her father, that he had taken time off to spend time with just her, and she had been grateful that he never mentioned the child.

She shook her head at her own predicament. She finally realised how much she had grown fond of Saralakka, and it actually warmed her heart.

***

She opened up to Soumya the next morning.

"You know, what you said made me think. I think it is more about having to compete with the child for Saralakka's affection. I thought I would be less hurt if I kept away."

"What makes you think Saralakka will stop paying you attention?"

Anupama shrugged.

"Anyway, I am in no hurry to go back home. I will stay at *ajji* and *thaatha's* place once I get back. I have a plan that I want to work on."

She continued, "Remember the village I spoke to you about during my PhD field work, the one with a dried-up lake, Karihalli? And the woman who shooed me away saying there was nothing to say as they had no water, so what was the point?"

Soumya nodded, curious.

"I have been thinking about it lately. I am planning to revisit the village."

Soumya nodded again as if prompting her to continue.

"I feel the urge to do something. It is such a shame that the lake there has been left to die. Such a huge one, too. The next village has clear water flowing down its canals. It is such a contrast."

Soumya was thoughtful. "There are so many things you need to work on."

Anupama nodded vigorously. "Yes, yes, of course. I have done a lot of thinking."

She was beginning to get excited about the idea.

"Well, keep me in the loop. And if you need help, Santhosh should be around. He has put in a request to be in Mysore."

"Great. How is he doing? Haven't seen him in years!"

"Oh, he is good. Busy as ever."

Santhosh was now a Collector in a district in North Karnataka.

***

On the flight back home, Anupama felt strangely light. She had learned and seen so much. More importantly, she had acknowledged to herself that she was indeed so fond of Saralakka that the new arrival made her insecure. Both feelings were a revelation to her, and all she could do was cross her fingers and hope for the best.

"And that is how it is going to be, until I tackle the Karihalli problem," she decided.

She and Soumya had a great time. They had said goodbye to each other with great affection and regret that they couldn't spend more time together. Soumya was the only one who had challenged her to look into herself and find answers for her behaviour, and she was grateful for that.

She was still in no mood to go back to a home with a new person in it. She couldn't imagine it; she was always the youngest at home and at both her grandparents' place, doted upon, protected.

She sent all the gifts, including the bag of frocks that her aunt gave, through Raghunath who picked her up at the airport and dropped her off at her grandparents'. He did not want to push her; he knew his daughter well enough to hope that this status quo would not last long.

Anupama showed the wedding pictures to her dad and grandparents and talked non-stop about her bus journey to Chicago. Raghunath and her grandparents sensed the lightness in her demeanour and hoped that the trip to the US had done her good.

***

"I *will* come home, *Appa*, but not now. I have planned a project. Let me complete it. Please give my enquiries to Saralakka."

Raghunath left for home, disappointed. Next time, he would have to have a talk with her, he decided.

***

Anupama got down to work immediately. She wanted some concrete plans ready so that she could discuss her ideas with Suma when she came. She put down on paper all that she thought should be worked on at Karihalli. But as the unhappy woman in the village had said, water was obviously at the top of the list.

Suma was excited about the idea.

"Let's do it, Ann," she exclaimed. Liam and Freja had shortened her Anno to Ann.

"I would like to start off alone, Suma. Let me see how viable this is."

"Cool. You just have to call me."

***

Day in and day out, Anupama pored over literature on lake and river cleaning, and the mind-boggling ways in which a village could be transformed.

Most important was where to stay and who to start with. Did she need permissions?

She would check out the situation and then decide on registration and other things, she thought.

She discussed at length with her grandfather and later with her dad on the phone. She wanted to keep this piece of information away from Venkat for some time. She sent Soumya a detailed email of all that she planned.

She went back to her PhD fieldwork diary to check for leads. She came across the name of the schoolmaster who taught at Karihalli— the children there had shown her the village school, closed that day.

She had luckily written down his name and the village where he came from.

The next day was a Sunday, and she set off to the village where the master lived. She got off at the town bus stand and took another bus that stopped at his village. The bus passed Madenahalli. She got off at the next stop and spoke to a group of men sitting at the bus stop.

"Could you tell me where to find Venu Master?"

"Take the first right; his house is at the end of the road."

Thanking them, Anupama set off towards her house. Having taken an early bus, she had reached the village by noon; she hoped to be able to get back by evening.

Venu Master's house was a small concrete building, cool and dark inside. Venu Master himself came to the door, which was already open, when she rang the bell.

"*Namaste*," she said. "Venu Master?"

***

They were soon in earnest conversation. His wife interrupted them with two cups of tea. A friend from the district office had approached Venu Master to take care of the new school at Karihalli a few years ago.

"No one from the surrounding villages wanted to teach there. Folks at Madenahalli did not let any teacher continue at Karihalli for long."

"How did you manage, sir?" Anupama asked with curiosity.

"Oh, I just avoided going into Madenahalli. There was no route in and out of Karihalli from the other side, like we have today. I cycled past Karihalli, took a U-turn and cycled back to Karihalli so no one would notice!"

"That's genius," laughed Anupama.

"Education is nobody's property," he commented, "and I have never regretted taking up the job."

When Anupama explained her plan, he was not so sure.

"I don't know if this will work, but I will support you in whatever you want to do."

"My first concern is to find a place to live in."

"I will take you to my cousin's house in the town after lunch. He will help you."

She gratefully accepted and sat for lunch with him and his two teenage sons.

***

Venu Master's cousin in the town was a government clerk at the town office. He took Anupama and Venu to a tiny one-room house with a kitchen and attached bath. It was new and clean, at the centre of the town, with all amenities close by. "This is a busy and safe area to live in, too. I will get you a reliable girl to help with housework if needed."

Anupama loved it. They met the owner, and she paid the advance rent. The owner insisted on meeting an elder from her family. She promised to get back the next week with her things, "and some elders as well", who, she knew would also

---

Namaste: An Indian way of greeting a person

insist on seeing the town and the house she picked to stay in. She had a lot of money saved, having been given dollars by both her brother and uncle for her expenses in Chicago, which she had hardly used. Besides, she had saved a lot of her own earnings, too.

***

CHAPTER EIGHT

The Project

It was not easy; she did not expect it to be easy. Karihalli was actually a small village of a little more than two hundred people with about 50 families. The dry lake divided Madenahalli and Karihalli; it always was part of Karihalli; the people of Madenahalli, who had canals full of water flowing throughout the year, dumped their garbage on this side of their village, polluting the lake, finally making it dry and dirty. The people at Karihalli struggled with just one good well in the village.

Madenahalli benefited from this; the men of Karihalli were forced to work in their fields, their own tiny plots lying unused.

***

Anupama worked over the weekend to set her house in order, and Prema, her new help, agreed to come early in the morning for work. She had college to attend at nine and the agreement was that she would leave from there itself, after both of them had breakfast.

On Monday, after an early shower, Anupama lit the lamp next to the picture of Lord *Ganesha*, both of which her grandmother had gifted for the new house. "*Vigneshwara*, help me," she prayed.

Prema was already there; she cleaned the house and the kitchen, made breakfast and lunch which she packed for the two of them, while Anupama hung the clothes that she had put in the machine out to dry. It was decided that Prema would make dinner in the evenings, finish her studies and homework, have dinner, and then leave for her house which was just a ten-minute walk away.

They left together after breakfast. Anupama took the bus, got off at Karihalli and walked to the school. The village was a good three or four kilometres away from the bus stop.

The bell had rung, and Venu Master was with the lower classes, having given the higher classes some assignments to work on. The school had students from class one to seven.

"Has anyone from Karihalli gone to town and studied till 10th class? Joined college?" she asked Venu Master.

"Maybe three or four boys as far as we know. They don't come to the village; they stay in the town."

Anupama kept an eye on the primary school children while Venu Master focused on the older children.

Some of them recognised her and exclaimed with happy surprise, "*Akka*, you are back! Are you going to teach us?"

"No, but I want to talk to you all after class. Don't run home. How many of you are in school, by the way?"

"Oh, we are so many of us!"

Ganesha/Vigneshwara: A popular Indian deity believed to be a remover of obstacles.

Murali Master gave her the details. "There are 67 children in this school. Most of them are in classes one to five. About 30 girls in all, none in the higher classes."

***

By noon, the village had heard of the "new person" and the women, elders, and smaller children gathered in front of the school to meet her.

Many of them had met her earlier, and they were happy to see her again.

"Welcome! Did you get your degree? Are you joining the school?"

"No, she is not," clarified Venu Master. "She has a proposal for you. The school is not part of it."

Venu Master closed the doors of the school, bid the children and Anupama goodbye, and left. He did not want the school to get into any trouble; it was important that classes went on regularly.

Anupama sat on the verandah and addressed the crowd.

"*Namaste*. Yes, I did get my degree, thank you! How have you all been?"

"Wrong question!" she thought, as the elders started complaining of cough, weakness, loss of appetite, declining eyesight… the complaints were never-ending!

"We will take care of all that. How is the water situation?"

"What to say… it is the same year after year."

"Don't you wish you could do something about it?"

"Like what?" asked one of them.

"Like probably clean the lake? Such a waste of a good water body, don't you think?"

"But the landlords will not allow it. Besides, who will do it? We need to go to work; our families need to have food to eat."

Some of the school children volunteered enthusiastically. She shook her head.

"No, not now. You have to attend school. Venu Master would not allow it."

Finally, some of the women, having discussed among themselves, turned to her. One of them asked her, "Are you sure we can do that? Won't we get into trouble with the landlords?"

"This is your lake, isn't it? And they don't use it anyway."

The women nodded. "Yes, it has been with us."

There was excitement among the women. "Imagine how good it would be to have a lake with water," they whispered. The men were not so sure, though.

"Why are you doing this? We don't want any trouble."

"Believe me, there will be no trouble. We will not disturb anybody."

The older men were still sceptical, "Let the others come home from the work in the fields," one of them said. "We need to discuss this."

Anupama agreed. Some of the older children took her to the lakeside. She walked around it, but she couldn't go close since it was not walkable. The lake was about 5-6 acres in area, and sufficient to take care of the needs of the village. She was quickly going through all that could be done and needed to be done in her mind. A few wells would also be great, she thought. She was confident that they would not need to dig deep to find water.

***

As she was leaving for the day, the women met her. "We were thinking, if we do not help ourselves, then who will? We have been going through this for as long as we can remember. The village officer or Tahsildar has not done anything to help us. They listen only to the landlords in Madenahalli."

Anupama was relieved. "Why don't we plan it out tomorrow? I will be here by 9 a.m. Finish your household work by then, and we will have a meeting."

***

The next morning, Venu Master called out to a boy in the seventh standard. "Shankara, ask your mother to spread a mat below the tree near the big well. They can have their meeting there."

Anupama reached Karihalli by nine and was happy to see that the women had already gathered near the well. She understood Venu Master's concern, and she herself did not want the school children to be involved, not at this stage, at least. Ramadevi, Shankara's mother, had spread out a few mats and also kept a jar of water nearby.

Anupama opened her laptop, and the women peeped in, curious. She showed them pictures of lakes being cleaned, lakes that were transformed after the cleaning. Why, people even cleaned beaches! The women were hopeful and excited.

The day wore on, and they tried to set out a schedule for work, the tools they would need, and distributed the work among themselves. After lunch, Anupama suggested they tour the small village, and they all did. There were small plots of land lying unused. They went to the lake and estimated the time it would take them to first clear the garbage and then work on desilting the lake.

"We need to build a bund and maybe plant some trees around the lake."

The men got back from work in the evening and met Anupama.

"Will you pay us for this?" one of them inquired.

Anupama had thought of this, but she did not have enough money to pay them for the work.

"No," she replied. "But I could go to the taluk office and find out if there are any funds."

The men were not convinced. "We men cannot lose our livelihood. Besides, even if the lake is cleaned, we would still need work."

Her best bet was the women, Anupama realised, and the men did not seem to mind the women doing the lake cleaning work. That was a good enough beginning, she thought; better than she hoped for!

***

Venu Master and his sons helped her buy the tools to be used to clean the lake. Anupama and the women sat together and drew up a schedule. The women wanted to start once the children and men left and work till lunchtime. It was long and arduous work, and the women, after an initial confusion, fell into a steady rhythm of clearing the garbage from the lake. Anupama had bought gloves for them all, and it helped. She realised that many of them had no footwear, so she decided to buy some rubber footwear of different sizes. That evening Prema and she shopped for footwear.

They worked with determination; for the women, this project seemed to be a godsend.

Back at home, Anupama worked hard, analysing the day's work and what could have worked better. A few weeks into the cleaning, they realised they still had a lot to do. New problems arose: where to dispose of the garbage, sorting the garbage, some of it was too dirty to be handled. People at Madenahalli heard of the lake cleaning work and came to watch out of curiosity. They laughed at the slow pace of work and were certain the women would abandon the work in a few days. Confident that it was doomed to fail, they ignored Anupama and the women.

The women worked hard. Anupama was touched by their confidence in her, and she admired their determination. They encouraged each other to work harder. Anupama decided to visit the taluk office and inquire about any possible funds. Venu Master's cousin took her to the officer in charge, shaking his head, saying that nothing would come of it.

And she found that he was right— but she persisted, and waited outside the Tahsildar's office for a meeting. When she finally did meet him, he told her, "Don't meddle in the affairs of the villages, miss. You are an educated girl, go back to the city and find yourself a job."

Looking at the expression of anger on Anupama's face, he continued, "Where is your licence? Are you a registered NGO?"

"I am on my own, here to help. I am using my own money. But I do realise that we need more. Are there any funds for the development of this area? Can you release some funds for Karihalli?"

"Things don't work like that, miss,"

"I may have to meet the Collector, then," countered Anupama.

"Be my guest," he replied sarcastically, "first get a licence and registration."

Anupama walked out furious.

She had a few visitors from Madenahalli that evening.

Prema opened the door to three men who asked for Anupama. They did not enter the house.

"Namaste, *Amma*. We are from Madenahalli. This is a request from our master to not interfere with our villages."

Obviously, the news of her visit to the town office had reached the landowners at Madenahalli.

"Thank you for coming all the way here. I will think about it."

The men left. Anupama shut the door and sat down on the chair, at a loss for words.

***

She needed some kind of official licence that could strengthen her case, and she decided to visit the District Collector's office.

"Next week," she thought. Meanwhile, she would do some research on all that she would require to place an application.

A sense of hopelessness engulfed her.

"Aargh…" she screamed suddenly, clenching her fists, scaring Prema. Prema had always seen a calm and committed woman, and she was concerned. She insisted on staying back with Anupama that night and made a quick call home to inform her mother.

***

Anupama set off to Karihalli the next morning. As she got off the bus, she noticed the three men who visited her the night before watching from a distance. She had enough experience with villages to be deterred by this and quickly walked down to the meeting place. She did not speak to anyone of the visit from the people of Madenahalli, and that day's work went on without interruption.

The next day, however, was different. The men had not yet left for the fields, and they were waiting for her with the womenfolk.

"*Namaste, Amma,*" they greeted her.

"*Namaste!* Have you decided to join us?"

"Our landlords have threatened to throw us out if we let you continue to clean the lake. Where will we go then?"

"First of all, they are the ones who need you all. Who will they get to do your work at such short notice? And don't you want to progress? Look at the world. Do you even know what is happening out there?"

The men were silent. They were in a predicament. They wanted their village to get out of its hopelessness. The women were ready for the change, but they had no courage to stand up to their landlords. Besides, who would bring food to the house?

The womenfolk refused to stop cleaning the lake, and the men left for their work at Madenahalli.

***

Things got worse.

She had just reached home when Venu Master knocked on the door.

Sipping the tea that Prema served, he told her there was more trouble.

"Some of the men were beaten up yesterday and told not to come back to work. It is going to be difficult for the poor folk. We need to think of some way of helping them out."

Anupama was upset and worried about the men. She did not have enough money to pay them for their work. She thanked Venu Master for the information. She gave him some money.

"Please send one of your sons to Karihalli to give this money to any one of them who needs to visit the doctor."

***

Her project was acquiring dimensions that she did not expect. She needed to get a licence and registration if she had to keep the Tahsildar from interfering. She had to get some funds so that she could pay the women and men, borrow machinery, and get work done faster. For all this, she would have to visit the District Collector's office immediately.

Anupama sat at the table, her bowed head supported by her hands, lost in thought. What if the landlords at Madenahalli threw all the Karihalli men out? She was aghast. They couldn't do that! It would be her fault if they did.

It was growing dark outside, and Prema was getting dinner ready. Anupama sat in the room, unmindful of anything. She did not hear it when the doorbell rang. Prema, who thought Anupama would answer the door, went on with her work. The bell rang again, and wiping her hands, Prema hurried into the room to open the front door. She switched on the light as she walked to the door, calling out to Anupama, "*Akka*, why are you sitting in the dark? Didn't you hear the doorbell ring?"

Anupama came out of her reverie and looked towards the door as Prema opened it. She had never been so happy to see anyone in her whole life as she was then; she was to declare later.

Suma stood at the door, grinning. "More than a month and no word from you!" she exclaimed as she walked into the house. "Are you going to invite me in or not? I am hungry!"

***

Anupama hugged her friend with joy. "How come?" she asked.

"I waited for you to call me. Since you did not, I thought I would drop in myself. Submitted my thesis, too, so I am jobless and homeless too!"

When they sat down, she said, "Seriously, now, I have great news."

Anupama could not imagine what it was. She just looked at Suma, waiting for her to continue.

"Remember the rural development project we applied for, only because Liam and Freja persuaded us to?"

"What? Are you saying it has been approved?" Anupama could not believe it.

"Of course, it has been approved! Liam mailed the approval letters and a cheque to boot to Prof. Ananthkrishna. Five lakh rupees, as an initial payment for the rural development project. The professor has given me a cheque in your name. They want us to register our project and open an account in the project's name so they can transfer the money."

"Oh my God!" Anupama exclaimed. "We asked for 25 lakh or some such amount, didn't we?"

"50 lakh rupees, you idiot. They told us to include all possible expenses, remember?"

Relief washed over her like a cool, exhilarating wave.

"Prema, can we all have dinner? I am hungry too," she called out.

"Let me get my bags and have a quick wash first," Suma said as she got up from her chair.

"Don't tell me you drove down!" exclaimed Anupama as she stepped out with her and grinned happily at the faithful old Maruti Zen parked in front of the house. Suma took out her bag and a small, nicely rolled quilt.

"Rushed here with just the basic stuff," she said as they walked in.

"We will drive to Mysore to deposit the cheque and visit the Collector's office tomorrow," Anupama said after dinner. "I just called Venu Master and informed him, so he can tell the womenfolk at Karihalli that I will not be going tomorrow."

She decided to inform her father once they got back to Karihalli.

"Okay!" Suma yawned as she rolled out her quilt and spread the sheet that Anupama gave her. She threw down a pillow, stretched herself out, and was soon fast asleep.

***

CHAPTER NINE
Anupama

They left early the next morning. By the time they reached the city, banks were open, and they drove straight to Anupama's bank, having stopped for breakfast on the way. Much as she would have liked to go home, Anupama had other pressing matters to attend to and wanted to go to the Collector's office first. Suma did not ask any questions, and after a quick coffee at a restaurant nearby, they drove down to the Collector's office.

The office gates were just opening up, and people were beginning to walk in. As they walked towards the office rooms, Anupama looked up at the signboard and gave a small exclamation, "Why, Santhosh is here!"

"My friend Soumya's brother!" she answered Suma's look of inquiry.

***

They walked into the office and requested to meet the Collector.

"Please wait, he will be here soon. You may have to wait some time."

Both of them sat down, ready to wait. They were thankful that the clerk had been approachable and helpful.

"It has been years since I saw him last. In fact, we haven't met since he passed the civil service exams. Of course, Soumya keeps sending me photos."

But when he came in, it was difficult to recognise the formally dressed young man who walked into his office without a glance at those who were waiting for a meeting with him.

It was almost an hour and a half later that she and Suma were called in.

Her "Good morning, sir," made him glance up.

"Why, Anupama! I almost did not recognise you! It has been years."

Anupama smiled and introduced Suma. Soon, she was explaining her situation to him. Santhosh was impressed with her work. His sister was always the brighter and bolder of the two friends, and it pleased him to see that Anupama was doing something so different with her life. He had heard about the new sibling; his mother and Soumya had told him.

"You apply for a licence, and I will allot some funds, too. Just put in an application with your proposal." He called for a clerk and told him to instruct them on how to get things moving.

"Mom and dad have moved back to Mysore now that I am here. Do drop in. Mom will be happy to see you," he smiled, handing over his card to her.

They thanked him and went out with the clerk.

Once they were out, they squealed with excitement.

"Finally!" Anupama exclaimed. "Hope things move well from here on."

There was work to be done in the city, and Suma offered to stay in the city and finish the formalities. They booked a room for her at a small, comfortable hotel. They had their lunch there and drove back home. They had fun trying out a name for their project and finally settled for *Abhivrudhi*, "Development. Don't you think it is apt?" Anupama asked, excited.

Suma left again for the city the next day with her luggage.

***

The womenfolk at Karihalli were relieved to see Anupama the next day. Her absence the day before had left them feeling unsettled; they had continued the work nevertheless. A few men from the other side came over and threatened them, but this made them more determined.

They gathered around Anupama, anxious but wanting to work.

Anupama wanted to meet the men who were beaten up the other day. It was important to speak to them. She walked into their homes and spoke to them.

"Take care," she said. "I met the Collector yesterday; he has promised to help us. He has even assigned two policemen on duty near Karihalli."

Santhosh had not told her this, but when she got off the bus at Karihalli in the morning, she had noticed two policemen patrolling the place.

***

Convincing the men to go ahead with the work was difficult. The women, though, even the ones from the families of the men who were attacked, were sure they wanted to go on. So, it was back to the women again. The men went to their landlords in Madenahalli and swore to continue to work for them, lake or no lake.

Anupama now had money to pay them, and she paid them on a daily basis. That weekend, she went back to the city, stayed with Suma, and on Monday, while Suma went to the registration office, she met Santhosh once again. She gave a detailed plan for the village.

"Some old wells to be reworked on, water pipes and at least two taps"— kitchen and bath, which meant toilets, cleaning up the unused land spaces for crops, or at least vegetables, some more classrooms, one more teacher, a small one-room house with a kitchen and toilet for whoever wants to stay there— the new teacher, anybody."

Santhosh smiled, "Well, that is ambitious, but not unachievable. I will get things moving. I shall send people and machines tomorrow to quicken the lake and well cleaning process too."

Anupama was satisfied.

"You know," she continued, "such a fertile area, and the landlords in Madenahalli created an artificial scarcity just so they didn't lose out on poor labour! How did the authorities miss it for so long? So close to the city, too."

"Right, we will definitely work on this. Come home for lunch?"

"Sorry, I am planning to leave with Suma by lunchtime."

"Okay! A quick coffee and snack then. I know a good place nearby."

Before she could say anything, he got up, went to the door, and opened it for her.

They crossed the street to the restaurant, and Santhosh ordered coffee. To Anupama, this was new, but she was comfortable with Santhosh, and she enjoyed herself.

They bade a friendly goodbye, and Anupama left for the hotel to wait for Suma.

***

Two days later, as Santhosh promised, two men arrived with a desilting machine. The folks at Karihalli were agog with excitement. There was more to come, though; a few hours later, Santhosh himself arrived with a few officials. Word spread that the Collector was at Karihalli. The men came running from the fields; never in their living memory had anything like this happened!

The Tahsildar and other town officers came rushing too.

Anupama and Suma did not expect this and were excited. They took Santhosh around the small village. His officers made notes as Anupama explained; the women helped her too.

Santhosh sat on the school verandah and addressed the school children and the women. The men walked in from the next village.

Santhosh spoke to Venu Master and agreed to get two more teachers and more classrooms.

"Who owns the land around the lake?" asked Santhosh.

Nobody answered; no one knew if it had owners at all.

"Are you ready to own it as a village and work together?"

"What do we do, sir? It is not large enough to grow crops."

"We will take it, sir," Sarojamma spoke up. She was a young housewife who had come from another village to Karihalli as a bride. "We will grow vegetables and sell them in the town."

The other women were excited and nodded their heads vigorously.

"Well, that is settled then," Santhosh ordered the officials to get a land record ready in the name of Karihalli Women's Collective; it would belong to all of them.

Santhosh left, giving orders for pipelines and toilets to the town officials. The villagers followed him all the way to his car, thanking him and blessing him along the way.

Anupama now had more time to focus on other matters. She called for a meeting of the women and discussed the logistics of the vegetable collective.

The women divided the work among themselves. Sarojamma was to take care of the accounts; she was a seventh standard 'pass'. Ramadevi and Vanaja were overall in charge. Ramadevi's husband, Muniyappa, and another elderly farmer, Chikkanna, were to transport the vegetables to the town and do the sales. Santhosh had promised them a co-operative shop.

***

Anupama and Suma were grateful and happy that things were going well.

"Finally!" exclaimed Anupama. She had never been this exuberant in life. "Since we don't have to spend on cleaning and laying pipes, we could spend on the school. And build a small one-room house for anyone like us who wants to visit there or for the new school teacher."

"Yes," agreed Suma.

Back home, Anupama texted a grateful thank you to Santhosh and sent a long email to Somwya and Raghunath.

With the Collector's direct intervention, things moved quickly. Venu Master was grateful and excited that the school was going to benefit from her project. His cousin in the town helped them get a good contractor, and work began. The town office also put out an advertisement for a new school teacher.

***

The Tahsildar was asked to check the payment given to the Karihalli farm labourers by the landlords in Madenahalli. The Collector fixed a rate for each farmer to be paid per month, along with enough produce every month. He wanted everything accounted for and kept in the office records.

Landlords in Madenahalli, who had kept a low profile, were enraged at this further interference in their age-old practice.

***

Work went on well at Karihalli. Suma stayed back home that morning since she had to pick up some things in the town that the building contractor had asked for. Anupama left by bus after breakfast. She joined the women in clearing up the vegetable plot. The women were hopeful and happy. They laughed and joked as they worked.

"Do you know the Collector personally, *Amma*?"

"Yes, we were neighbours as children."

"He seems to like you."

"Of course, he does!" said Anupama.

"Oh, so you know!"

"What is there to know?"

The women giggled. "What?" asked Anupama and suddenly blushed, making the women laugh.

She left a little after four, as usual. She started walking down the three-kilometre stretch to the main road. She was so used to this now that the distance hardly mattered. It was on the other side of Madenahalli— some stretches open; she could see fields in the faraway villages, some stretches covered with trees lining the rough mud road on either side.

***

It was too late to run or protect herself when it happened. She found herself surrounded and attacked by stick-wielding men. She fell to the ground, hurt and bleeding in the head. The men surrounded her, kicked her savagely, and finally left, satisfied, when she went limp and unconscious. She lay there for more than an hour, going in and out of consciousness. The pain was unbearable; her sight became hazy. She had no option but to lie there and hope that someone would finally miss her and come looking for her.

***

Venu Master had already left. The lake desilting workers parked their machine at 5 p.m. and left for the day.

Suma received the call a little after five. She and Prema rushed to the village. The villagers had gathered around Anupama; she was propped up, leaning on Ramadevi, conscious, battered, and bleeding. Ramadevi gently made her sip some water, and they waited for Suma to arrive. They carefully put Anupama in the back seat of the car, Prema supporting her head on her lap. Muniyappa sat in front, and they rushed back to the town. Prema called Venu Master and told him of the attack. By the time they reached the town hospital, Venu Master's cousin was there, waiting for them. The duty doctor helped arrest the bleeding. "But she needs to be taken to the city hospital immediately," he said and called for the driver of the lone ambulance that was fortunately free to get ready for the journey.

Meanwhile, Suma called Santhosh and Raghunath from Anupama's phone.

It was a long drive for Suma and Muniyappa, who insisted on accompanying her. Anupama kept coming in and out of consciousness. It was late in the night when they reached the city, and Santhosh had everything ready and waiting at the hospital. Raghunath was there, too.

Raghunath stayed back at the hospital outside the ICU where Anupama was admitted. Early next morning, Sarala came to the hospital after which Raghunath left. Sarala's father, Chinnappa, had reached the previous night, and she could now leave the child at home under his care. Suma left with Muniyappa the next morning; she knew Anupama would have wanted her in the town.

Anupama battled it out for a week in the ICU, alternating between consciousness and unconsciousness. The doctors had to perform an emergency surgery to stitch up her ruptured intestine; she had fractured her rib cage, and the wound on her head needed stitches.

***

The town police, meanwhile, made their inquiries and arrests at the Collector's orders; a few goons who attacked her at a landlord's behest. Sarala stayed outside the ICU, going home only to bathe and change. Raghunath came in every evening, directly from work. Santhosh dropped in daily.

Finally, Anupama was declared fit enough to be shifted to the ward. Still weak and groggy with all the drugs, her senses were yet to get coherent. Sarala refused to leave her side and tended to her day and night.

"No, don't bring the little one here. I want to focus fully on Anupama. *Appa* and Gowri will take care of her well," she said when Raghunath suggested he bring the little one to the hospital.

Santhosh dropped by every evening, sometimes accompanied by his parents, or to pick up his mother who happened to have gone earlier to see Anupama.

***

"Saralakka, is that really you?" A weak voice spoke to her one evening, and Sarala looked up with happy relief. Anupama was looking at her, wondering.

"Yes, *Putti*, it is me." Then she joked, "Don't tell me you have forgotten how I look!"

Anupama smiled gently, but unable to say anything more, closed her eyes and went back to sleep. She slept through the evening and night, and Sarala sat in vigil, not moving from her bedside, lest she miss her waking voice.

Of all of them, Sarala knew why Anupama left, and she had waited for her, letting her take her time. But the savage attack on her changed everything. She knew she had to be by Anupama's side at this hour.

Anupama had a special place in her heart, and not even her own little girl could take that away from her. She had been by her side as Anupama grew from a heartbroken eight-year-old girl into a mature and intelligent woman. They gave each other company in their loneliness, and their bond, silent, unexpressed, why, even unknown, had only grown stronger over the years. Anupama was her friend, teacher and yes, a beloved daughter.

She refused to leave until Anupama, two days later, woke up as if refreshed from a deep sleep. Sarala looked up from her book to see Anupama watching her. Their joy in acknowledging each other was dramatic, great, and mutual. After many tears and embraces, Sarala called Raghunath, Santhosh, and Suma.

***

Finally, that night, at Anupama's insistence, Sarala left for home, promising to get back the next morning as early as possible.

Raghunath stayed back, and Santhosh had just left, promising to come the next day too.

When Sarala came the next morning, Anupama was still asleep. Raghunath left, saying he would be back in the evening. Whether he should bring the little one was left unasked and unanswered between them.

When Anupama woke up, she looked around and asked, "Saralakka, where is the baby?"

"Oh, she is at home with *appa* and Gowri; she will be fine."

"Is Chinnappa here, too? Please call *appa* and ask him to bring both of them this evening, Saralakka,"

Sarala did not show her emotions. She called Raghunath and told him to bring Chinnappa and the little one in the evening.

Both were excited and anxious; both had the same question in their minds: "Will she like the child?"

The child was more than a year old and had learned to walk on her own.

It was time for their arrival, and Santhosh had just come in with his parents. Raghunath arrived right after they did, with the child and Chinnappa.

Sarala took the child in her arms and walked towards Anupama, who was propped up in bed.

Anupama looked at the child, amazed. "Why, she looks just like me!" she exclaimed in utter disbelief.

Both daughters had taken after Raghunath; there was no denying it.

Sarala laughed, partly relieved, partly proud.

"Hello, what is your name, baby?" Anupama asked, stretching out her hand to hold the child's hand.

"Nirupama, named after your grandmother, and rhyming with yours," Sarala beamed.

Anupama smiled a happy smile. After how long, she did not know.

The child was duly introduced to Santhosh and his parents. Chinnappa sat by Anupama and made his inquiries.

Sarala sent a boy with a flask, asking him to buy tea for everyone. Anupama's evening tea was about to arrive. The child walked around, the bells in her little anklets ringing gently as she did.

Santhosh came by Anupama's bed.

"Finally," he smiled. "How are you feeling? You scared us all."

Anupama smiled back at him. "Actually, I am feeling great," she said, looking around the room. There was so much life and cheer in it.

She held out her hand to thank him. "You have been a great support. I cannot thank you enough."

Santhosh held her hand. "I have great respect for what you are doing, Anupama. You put us officials to shame. There is so much to do."

"Yes. But once Karihalli is settled, I am getting back to academics!" she smiled, looking at Sarala and her father.

"Planning to get back home? That is great. Stay with me, marry me."

It was so unexpected that Anupama was silent. Her hand continued to remain in his; she remembered the teasing by the village women and the happy feeling she felt when she realised what they were hinting at.

She surprised herself with a "Yes, I would love that! That's a great idea."

They laughed.

***

CHAPTER TEN
A New Beginning

Muniyappa sat by the lake. He refused to sleep or even stay indoors; he could not. The night was dark. The moon glowed weakly behind cloudy skies. The monsoon was fast approaching. The season's first rains were yet to come, though. He prayed for a miracle, as he did every night since Anupama came into their lives. He was grateful that they accepted her and were willing to work with her. The lake bed was clean and wet with puddles here and there, thanks to the mild pre-monsoon showers.

"After all, she need not have bothered," he thought.

"Who did, ever?" His mind asked him. No one, at least, not till today, not that he could remember.

How clean the place was! Did he even dream that one day he would be sitting here?

Shankara came looking for him.

"Let's go home, *Appa*," he said, settling down beside his father. "No, Shankara. We have done all we can. It is time."

Shankara sighed.

"What are you waiting for, *Appa*?" he asked.

"I don't know, Shankara, I don't. A miracle?"

Shankar laughed. "A miracle? After all that we went through? With Anupama *akka* so ill?"

Muniyappa was silent.

***

Anupama was in the hospital for a month. Her grandparents came to see her; Venkat called her every day once he got the news from them. She was relieved that he was told only after she got better; he would have been in an uncomfortable predicament had it been otherwise. It was the same with Soumya. Initially upset, she was euphoric when Anupama told her that Santhosh had proposed to her.

"Whaaat?" she screamed at the other end of the phone. "Yes, yes, yes!"

***

Anupama refused to go back home yet, after the doctors said she could be discharged. Suma was visiting her every weekend, and things were good at the village. She wanted to go back.

"Let me finish my project. I need to get back."

Suma nodded, "The new house in Karihalli is ready, as are the extra rooms in the school. The wells have been dug and cleared of the old water. We used machines, connected pipes, and drew the old water out. The pipes will be laid for the houses; we will start with the new house."

"We could shift to the new house tomorrow, Suma," Anupama said, excited.

Suma left to get the house ready for Anupama, and Santhosh drove her back to Karihalli the next day. Venu Master and his sons helped Suma move their belongings to the village that Prema had already packed by the time Suma reached.

The villagers waited for Anupama; she had no clue of the enthusiastic welcome she would get.

The house was ready. There were flowers on the doorway and green mango leaves that were tied on a string stretched across the top of the front door. One of the women helped Anupama out of the car and gave her a bowl of water to wash her feet. Ramadevi stood at the entrance of the house; she welcomed her in with a traditional lighted lamp and adorned her forehead with vermillion *kumkum* powder, applying it carefully in a perfect circle.

The villagers cheered at this and gathered in front of her when she sat on the chair on the verandah. Santhosh was welcomed too, and he sat with her. Each of them, including the children, wanted to know how she was, if she was better, and the older ones blessed her.

***

That night, inside the tiny house, Anupama was already asleep. It had been a week since they shifted to the village, but Anupama was yet to step out and see for herself how well the project had progressed.

The night wore on. Sitting by the lake, Muniyappa still refused to go home. Shankar stretched out on the earth next to his father and fell asleep.

***

Muniyappa thought he was dreaming. He could see the reflection of the weak moon in the lake. He looked up and stretched his hands out to the skies. "Dear God, do something. Am I dreaming?" he cried.

He looked back into the lake, now down on his knees and hands, with his neck stretched out.

Water was seeping across the lake from deep down. The lake was alive!

Muniyappa shook his son awake. Shankar watched with awe, "Your miracle, *Appa*," he whispered.

"Tell the others; I will inform *amma*," Muniyappa ran towards Anupama's house.

"*Amma*," he knelt down by her bed and called out, unable to control his excitement, "Water."

Suma, who was still up, looked up from her book, wondering.

"Water," repeated Muniyappa. "The lake has water!"

"Finally!" exclaimed Suma joyously, putting her book down on the bed.

Anupama, now awake, smiled and whispered, "Help me to the lake."

Muniyappa and Suma gently helped her up and supported her as she walked out.

People were hurrying towards the lake, and children were running, excited. There were only a few in that crowd who had actually seen water flowing in the lake, but how long ago, they could not say.

The village danced and drummed when the first rains came.

***

Their work at the village was done, and it was time to move.

"Professor Ananthakrishna is taking over the project," Suma said. "He is excited. The project funds will be used to help villages improve their schools."

Anupama was happy.

As for Suma, Liam and Freja had invited her to Sweden, and she was leaving for Stockholm the next month. In the meantime, she planned to stay with her grandparents in Bangalore.

"When is the wedding?" she asked Anupama.

"Oh, not for another year. I need to get a teaching job and recover fully. Eva said she will definitely be there, hopefully with Venkat. Soumya says she will come with Mohit."

Both looked forward to the future, but the fact that their days of working and living together were coming to a close made their hearts heavy. They had grown close to each other and the village, and they would miss everything.

***

They planned to move out in a week, and though upset about their decision, the villagers knew it was time for them to take care of themselves.

Each house brought them food: it was either breakfast, lunch, tea, or dinner. They enjoyed the food, and "the fact that we don't have to cook!" laughed Anupama. The school children made small gifts and 'we love you' cards; invited them both to school one day and gifted it to them amidst great fun and fanfare.

Anupama and Suma drove down to the town to Prema's house and gave her a scholarship from their funds to complete her education. They met Venu Master's cousin at his office and thanked him.

Venu Master had invited them to dinner, and they drove to his house.

"Welcome," Venu Master's wife ushered them in with a warm smile. His sons were there, too.

They all sat together as one big family, ate, spoke, and laughed.

When it was time to go, his wife said, "Please wait," and went into her room.

She came out with a saree for each, and at their look of surprise, she said,

"Our gift for you two. Please don't say no!"

She gave each one a saree and some fruits, made them wear flowers in their hair, and gave them the vermillion *kumkum* powder and turmeric to adorn their foreheads.

***

That night, once they got back home, Anupama and Suma sat up talking for a long time. It would be a new beginning for each of them, and both were filled with hope for their future.

"I could not have asked for more," Anupama reflected. "To know that I am so much loved by my parents; dad and Saralakka; means everything. I have been running away all these years, from home, from myself." She shook her head with relief at how things turned out.

***

Raghunath drove over the next morning to pick her up. Anupama and Suma packed only their personal belongings; they left everything else in the new house.

"So that we can keep visiting," they joked.

Anupama had one last meeting with the women.

"Thank you for trusting me and supporting me so readily. Karihalli is indebted to its brave womenfolk. Take care of your village, your children, your waters, and your vegetables!"

The women laughed.

"This is your office from now on," Anupama continued, "for the Karihalli Women's Collective." The women applauded joyously, excited and happy. She gave the key to Ramadevi for safekeeping.

"I may not be in the village, but I am close by. Just call me if you need me. Even otherwise, I will definitely come to see you all."

It was a happy parting; the villagers bid an affectionate and grateful goodbye to Anupama and Suma.

***

They were to drive together till Mysore, from where Suma would continue to Bangalore. They stopped for lunch on the way. It was almost two when they reached Mysore, and Suma still had a long way to go.

They parted affectionately when they reached Mysore.

"Bye for now, Ann. I will come before I leave for Sweden," Suma promised.

As they drove down their street, Anupama's heart thudded with excitement and happiness. She was back, after years of physical and emotional running!

Sarala was at the door, waiting. She welcomed her with the traditional *aarthi*, applied the vermillion *kumkum* powder on her forehead, and put some sugar in her mouth as a sign of happy times to come. Both women glowed in their renewed, newfound, and newly expressed bond for each other as Anupama held Nirupama's outstretched little hand and stepped across the threshold into the house.

She had finally found herself. She was home.

***

Epilogue

The wedding was scheduled for May, almost a year after Anupama was offered a faculty position at a well-known city college. The coronavirus took over the world, and life went into a lockdown.

The college shut down before the semester examinations could begin. Anupama did not get to meet Santhosh as usual. Busy like never before, being out on work as a senior administrator, he did not visit her for fear of infection. A May wedding was impossible, and during one of their video chats, they decided to put it off for the time being.

Anupama, now completely recovered, spent her days helping with housework, completing her academic tasks, and playing with the little one. Raghunath was at home, too.

She worried about Venkat and Eva. Eva was pregnant and was due for delivery any time, and the US was one of the worst-hit countries. One night in the last week of May, in the wee hours of the morning when the house slept, Anupama's phone rang.

Venkat had made a video call to tell her that Eva had given birth to a boy and that both were fine. What with the COVID-19 pandemic and the 'I Can't Breathe' protests against the death of Black American George Floyd, they had been through hell trying to find a safe hospital. He could not hide his emotions and stuttered, "Is that *appa*?" when he saw Raghunath come into Anupama's room to check who the call was from.

Anupama silently handed the phone to Raghunath, and both father and son wept. There was no talk, and Anupama took the phone from her father's hand. "Congratulations to you both! I am so happy! Take care and call when you are both home with the baby."

And sure enough, the next day, Venkat called back, this time with Eva and baby in tow. Anupama and Raghunath talked to them for a long time; it was like holding on to the rainbow of hope. Nirupama could not contain her curiosity and sat on Raghunath's lap to peer into the laptop.

"Oh my God, that's like seeing Anno all over again!" Venkat could not help exclaiming.

"I know, right?" Anupama said, excited.

Sarala did not interfere. In her usual discreet way, she kept away from the family reconciliation that was a long time coming.

***

The COVID-19 situation was getting worse in India, and Anupama got busy with webinars and faculty development programmes. She worried for her students and for school children, with everyone talking of online classes and lectures. What would children and schools that did not have digital access do, she wondered.

She called Venu Master to find out how things were going on at Karihalli. Of course, they needed a few computers. Most houses had only basic mobile phones.

Soon after talking to Venu Master, she called Prema.

"Please arrange for a computer in each class. And train both the teachers in the basics," she requested.

The Karihalli Women's Collective was encouraged to stitch masks to be given to every household in the village and sell the remaining in the town. Sewing machines were transported from the city by the city administration.

***

Suma was still in Sweden and kept in touch. Soumya and Mohit, as frontline doctors, were extremely busy. Anupama worried for their safety, too.

The lockdown was lifted in phases, and it was during one of these phases that the families decided to conduct the marriage.

Santhosh said, "You will only be shifting from your house to mine. We could get married tomorrow!"

Since a regular wedding was out of question, it was decided that it would happen at the bride's house. Only her grandparents, Venkat and Suma; Liam and Freja; Soumya and Santhosh's close aunts and uncles were informed of the wedding.

***

As the lockdown was lifted, Anupama decided to make a trip to Karihalli. Thanks to the new confidence born out of the cleaning of the lake and the success of the Women's

Collective, people of Karihalli handled the pandemic with stringent preventive measures.

"Being isolated, for a change, has proved beneficial!" Muniyappa joked when Anupama appreciated the success of the Karihalli villagers in keeping the virus at bay. Ramadevi and others proudly showed the work they were doing— they stitched and sold masks to retailers in the town. The vegetable plots were lush and colourful; the produce was enjoyed by every household in the village.

Prema was with Anupama, and they stayed back for lunch at Muniyappa's house. They enjoyed the green countryside and then sat by the lake in the shade of a tree.

Prema was now a familiar figure at Karihalli; she coordinated with converting the classes to smart classes and brought in two temporarily out-of-work tailors from the town to teach the women tailoring once the machines came. Only two were allowed to learn at a time, since the room was small and they had to maintain social distance.

Soon, it was time to leave. Anupama dropped off Prema at her house in the town and drove back home, deep in thought.

She wondered about this invisible virus, which had brought the world down on its knees. She wondered what the future would bring. She hoped that the vaccines that countries across the world were working on would help them go back to the old times. Would children keep their masks on while they were outside? It was so uncomfortable! How would her students adjust to virtual classrooms? She had attended innumerable webinars where they discussed the pros and cons of virtual learning as the 'new normal'. "Fingers crossed," she thought, "hopefully the vaccine will be an answer to our prayers and hopes." She felt sorry for the little ones who were supposed to begin schooling in 2020 and the final-year college students who were supposed to graduate in 2020. Professor Ananthakrishna emailed her with the details of the village digital project he planned as part of the *Abhivrudhi* project.

2020 was a happening year, no doubt! Her thoughts went to the unprecedented protests against racial discrimination in the US and the controversy over J.K. Rowling's 'homophobia'. Why, she grew up on Harry Potter books! It was Venkat who went out with *amma* and bought the first one at the local bookstore. And both he and Anupama were hooked on the series. But the first Harry Potter film she saw was The Prisoner of Azkaban, and she did not miss any Harry Potter film after that. Soumya and she cajoled Soumya's mom to take them to the theatre to watch the films. Of course, she watched the first two on television later on.

Amma had introduced her to so many books. Venkat had a vast collection by the time Anupama grew old enough to read on her own. She had lost count of the number of times her mother read Thumbelina and Peter Rabbit stories to her! She told her many, many folk tales of her language, too, in a sing-song voice. And her collection of Amar Chitra Kathas was precious. How thrilled they both were when Anupama brought home the collection of Grimm's fairy tales from her school library! She and her mother took turns reading the stories aloud to each other.

Anupama smiled, thinking of her mother.

***

She would wear one of her mother's sarees for the wedding, she decided. Even the silk she wore for Venkat's wedding was *amma's*. She sat down in the room that evening, with Nirupama playing by her side. She spread a clean sheet on the floor and gently brought down her mother's sarees from the cupboard. Of course, *amma* wore beautiful sarees! Cottons, handlooms, silks; they were of beautiful hues and designs. She slowly went through the lot, her memories awakening with every saree that she caressed and put back in the cupboard— the beautiful peacock blue silk, which she had made *amma* promise she would keep for her, the white and red Bengali cotton, which made Anupama gaze at her mother whenever she draped herself in it, the lovely mustard and green silk, which *ajji* gave *amma* for Anupama's naming ceremony. She found a beautiful green silk which her mother seemed to have gotten all ready to wear, but had not.

"Saralakka," she called out, and when she came, she showed her the saree. "I am wearing this for the wedding. I have a lovely blouse, too, to go with it."

"That's beautiful," said a harried Sarala, getting little last-minute things done for the wedding that was happening in two days.

"Come in here, Saralakka, and sit down," Anupama patted the floor next to her.

"Did you decide what you will wear?" she asked her.

"Yes, *Putti*. I have kept out some new clothes for the little one too."

Anupama opened the safe and took out her mother's jewellery. Nirupama's eyes fell on the shiny jewels, and she came quickly towards her.

"Let's finish off with this, shall we?" Anupama said, ignoring Sarala's protests. Sarala sat down and quickly took Nirupama onto her lap, before the little one could put her hand in the box.

Anupama took out the beautiful jewellery that Raghunath's mother had gifted Latha during the wedding and later on.

"These are *ajji's*. They are yours now, Saralakka."

Her childhood jewels, small and cute, she gave to Nirupama. "I wouldn't wear them anyway," she said, ignoring Sarala's protests.

"My regular jewellery and the ones that *amma* brought from her house, I will keep and give some to Eva."

She put them in a smaller box and gave the big one to Sarala. "Keep them, Saralakka, and don't say no."

She packed just two suitcases of clothes to take with her initially. She had a lot of books and her college materials to pack, and her beloved laptop.

"Anyway, I can carry some of my clothes every time I visit," she said.

***

That night, she had a surprise email from Suma, who was still stuck in Stockholm. They either texted or called on WhatsApp almost every day, and Anupama was curious to see an email from her.

'Hi Ann,

Stockholm is a beautiful city! I feel so grounded here. The country is drawing flak for the way it is handling the pandemic, but I can't help loving it here.

All my adult life, I have been living the life of a nomad, with only my car for company. Dad and mom divorced when I was 15, and I stayed back with dad till he married a few years later. Mom had already married a colleague who was a divorcee with kids. Once dad also married, I went to my parents only when they were free to have me in their respective homes; I had to fall back on my grandparents at other times. You were one of the first people to have had a calming effect on my life and gave me a sense of purpose. How great was it, working at Karihalli! I felt at home there too:) I did not have to ask to come to your house in the town, and the villagers welcomed us at all times.

I wish to do so much. I wish to see the world, but not alone, not without a base to call mine. I am not visiting my parents any longer. They are welcome to come stay with me whenever they wish and wherever I am!

Liam and Freja are helping me apply for jobs here, tough during the pandemic times. I know. I don't even have a work permit.

Liam jokes that maybe I should marry him; that would be a great way to keep me here! Sometimes I wonder if I should say yes! Maybe we are all under the influence of your wedding celebrations. But then hey, what is life without having someone nice to share it with and settle down? Liam knows me better than anyone else, and I think that he kind of likes me!

So maybe I will go ahead and say yes the next time he 'proposes'!

What do you say?

Suma.'

"What would I say? What is there to say? I would say yes!" wrote back Anupama. "My house will always be open and welcome, whenever, however many times. So, three strong bases: my house, your grandparents', and your own house! Follow your heart; I know it will take you to your destiny. Lots of love! I wish we could all meet!"

***

Everyone seemed to be in a nostalgic mood.

Soumya, busy with frontline work, made a quick call the next morning.

"I will fly down as soon as the flights open up. How can I even miss this wedding? Please make sure you guys take lots of pics."

Anupama kept her DSLR camera to charge. Raghunath would take the pics; it was decided.

Santhosh's mother spoke to a priest to conduct the wedding.

Sarala got all the pooja things ready for the big day. The wedding was to be held at 11 a.m., and after an early lunch, Santhosh had to rush to work; Anupama would go to his house with his parents. Not wanting any fuss with too many people around, Sarala decided to make lunch for all of them.

The wedding guests consisted of Santhosh and his parents. The priest, of course, was an additional member.

Venkat called at least three times that day, "Just to talk." Her grandmother called and tearfully wished she was around, but of course, they could not travel from Bangalore. That evening, Anupama and Raghunath sat talking for a long time. Anupama remembered how neither she nor Venkat were there for his wedding with Sarala so many years ago. How far they had travelled since those troubled days! She would miss her grandparents, Venkat and his family, her uncle and aunt in the US, Soumya and Suma; Liam and Freja. They would dearly miss Chinnappa; there was no way he could travel all the way from the village.

Anupama, Raghunath, and Sarala continued to sit together long after dinner. Nirupama had fallen asleep on the sofa, listening to their soft voices. Sarala and Anupama applied *mehendi* on each other's palms. Both were good at drawing intricate *mehendis*, something they learned together when Anupama was a little girl.

Sarala had planned a simple vegetarian festival menu, with two traditional sweets thrown in.

Finally, Raghunath insisted that she and Sarala get the much-needed sleep, and they retired to bed.

***

That night, Anupama dreamt of her mother, young, beautiful, cheerful; happy for her; she dreamt that her mother and she went shopping for the wedding, just the two of them. She smiled in her sleep as they made this vague salesman in a vague, light-filled, colourful shop pull out saree after saree.

It was so many years ago, but her mother's memory was still fresh in Anupama's mind. Her mother would always remain young to them, she realised. Venkat was luckier; he had had a longer time with her.

"I have known *amma* for seven years longer than you do!" he used to tease her. "It was just *amma* and me, without you, you interfering little kid." While Anupama protested, her mother would only put her arm around her shoulder and laugh.

***

The household was up by four; there were so many little things to be done. Sarala got the pooja requirements ready. Raghunath swept and mopped the house from room to room, till it sparkled. Anupama made a quick breakfast for all of

---

Mehendi: A green herbal paste made from the leaves of the plant mehendi, used to adorn the palms during festivities, especially marriages.

them. She strung garlands of green mango leaves and lovely marigolds across the pooja room door and the front door. By seven, Sarala and Raghunath were in the kitchen, getting lunch ready. There was so much togetherness at home that Anupama did not mind she was running errands on her wedding day. Sarala and she had already kept the little one's clothes and jewellery out; Sarala's saree had been chosen; Anupama's saree and jewellery were carefully laid out on the bed in her room.

By nine-thirty, Anupama had had her breakfast, bathed, and wrapped the saree around her. She had worn her *jhumkhas* and a simple necklace with matching green and pink stones, along with matching bangles. She made up her face with a natural look; she looked beautiful and glowed.

Sarala tied Anupama's hair into a pretty bun at the nape of her neck and decorated it with a string of fresh jasmine flowers around it, pinning a lovely stone-studded gold flower at the centre of the top knot. Sarala was used to doing this for Raghunath's mother, and she did it beautifully.

***

When the groom and his parents arrived, everything was set, and the priest was already present There was love and happiness in the house. Sarala and Raghunath were quiet with emotion; the little one danced around in her finery. The wedding was over in an hour's time.

And so it was that with the world reeling under the pandemic, Anupama and Santhosh exchanged garlands and had a wedding like no other: beautiful, warm, and intimate, with the promise of a new beginning.

***

Jhumkas: Traditional Indian earrings.